Mavis was born within ti
Mavis liked to think they rang in her birth —
Her head butting blind and bloody into this wide and
wondrous world.

How wide and wondrous, how puzzling and joyful, challenging and dismaying she would discover as she went through childhood, adolescence, marriage, and sought to find her true self.

What were the circumstances of her conception?

Who was her father?

Who were the women who came to the door and from whom she had to be hidden?

Did her favourite aunt commit murder?

How is she to square reality with dreams of romance?

The search for answers makes an intriguing and compelling story told with pace in precise and vigorous prose, not a word wasted. The characters, the situations are specific and perused from differing viewpoints, but the themes are timeless and will stir memory and reflection moving readers to see afresh their own experiences.

See the Pretty Red Balloon

KATE MURRAY

PENTALPHA
PUBLISHING
EDINBURGH

CONTENTS

See
the
Pretty
Red
Balloon

1

Birthday Bells 1940

Mavis was born within the sound of Bow Bells. Mavis liked to think they rang in her birth: '*Pu-ush*!' Her head butting blind and bloody into this wide and wondrous world. The torso and limbs of her slithering out on the last stroke of the last hour. Midnight baby.

Upended, ankles finger-manacled: a buttock-slap! And 'Waa-aagh!' sings the daughter of Emily Stonebridge and 'Father: Unstated'.

Whatever happened to Emmie Stonebridge? The mother? Who named her baby 'May Emily'.

'*She*' adoptive Dad would call her – on the very odd occasion he had to call her something. Mind, if ever Mavis said '*she*' about anybody there'd be a telling-off from her mum: ''*She*' is the cat's mother.'

So. Miaow!

2

Wedding Bells 1960

'Happy is the bride the sun shines on.'

Yes! That box ticked. Cloudless sky. High sun.

'Something old, something new, something borrowed, something blue.'

Again, yes! Peeking out from the top of Mavis' bra is a white damask hanky edged with lace crocheted by her late mum; her bridal gown is new, her silver pendant borrowed from her Aunt Zilla, and cornflowers stud the white roses entwining the bandeau of her veil.

The bride is all set.

Wedding-bells swing.

But their clang and clamour should send her running from this place. Running screaming. Running for her life. Over the hills and far away.

Why?

Because the tip of the bridegroom's nose is unusually bulbous.

Because the bridegroom's eyes are somewhat protuberant.

Because small mounds pad the tops of his high-set cheekbones.

Aaagh!'

How can our bride have paid no heed to these portents? She, who has so often flinched goose-fleshy away from that same nudging nose? She, whose most unfortunate encounters with bald pates, buttocks, breasts in one shape and form or another have rendered globophobic'?

Blame bedazzlement by diamond-fire: signifying *chosen*. Blame beguilement by golden band-gleam: signifying *forever and ever*.

Woe! Woe!

3

Mavis. Summer 1946

It's sunny. But I'm not out skipping. I forgot and said 'Can I?' and Mum scrunched her face like she does when she's going to say, 'You *can*. The question is, whether you *may.*' But this time she didn't say that. She said, not now I couldn't because they'd got something to tell me. *They*! Must be something very special if it's Mum *and* Dad. Talking to me *together* – in the Christmas-only front room! Sitting side-by-side on the settee, Mum on the edge so's her feet touch the floor.

They're telling me they're not my real Mum and Dad.

Telling me they're not my Mum and Dad.

They don't say 'real Mum and Dad'; they say new words: 'evacuee' and 'adopted'.

'Evacuee.' That's the one I like. It's got four bits. And the first bit and the last bit both go 'ee'. And 'cause I'm saying 'eee-vacu-eee' in my head over and over and over I don't hear their words hardly at all. And when I do I don't know what they're talking about. Something about bombs, London and a bad man, Hitler.

'She didn't want you.'

'She'? Who's 'she'? A 'she' who didn't want … *me*?

It was Dad said it. Dad's voice is horrible and it's pulling at my eyes and punching little sore holes in my cheeks and my chest. Crying holes.

Now Mum's given Dad one of her looks. She hates his rough speaking. My mum's voice is nice and kind and soft: 'You were *chosen*. We chose *you*, my duck. We couldn't have any babies ourselves. We adopted you.'

'*Chosen*.' That's good, chosen. But, 'adopted'? I don't know that. I don't know anything about that. The words have got one, two, three and four bits. I put them in order: 'chose,' 'chosen,' 'adopted,' 'evacuee.'

'She was no good.'

That's my dad again. Snarly voice.

Mum takes a big breath in and blows it out quiet and long through her nose. Dad goes on – 'Now you're ours, my duck. You had your first birthday here with us, duck.' His voice all squashed out of shape now, all furry, as if he's eaten chalk like the Big Bad Wolf pretending to be Mother Goat so the kids will open the door and he'll gobble them all up. Dad's nodding now, looking all proud about what he said. I don't know why. You wouldn't go somewhere else for your first birthday, would you? You couldn't. Not a baby. That's stupid.

Next morning it's just Mum and me. Dad's gone early on his bike. To Old Millsons where it's all dark and red with scorchy yellow-blue fire and orange sparks struck everywhere and banging clanging echoes so you have to put your hands over your ears. I don't like that. I get frightened. I never want to go there with him. But I do like when I go and it's my birthday and he gives me a bunch of red balloons.

Some places we go, I like. One Sunday I was perched on the seat in front of Dad on his bike. It was miles and miles. He said we'd see a great big house and he lifted me right up on top of his shoulders but the house was behind lots of trees and I couldn't see it. And big, big high gates all curly at the top I saw. Dad said he made them, those gates. I didn't know how he could have. Those gates were a long way from our house and a long way from Old Millsons.

Round the gates were all lovely red and pink rhododendrons. I can spell them. You say 'roady' but it's spelt 'rhodo'. And 'encyclopaedia' I can spell. When there's grown-ups Dad says 'Spell 'encyclopaedia'.' I go 'e-n-c-y-c…' and I'm not hardly finished before Dad says 'She can it spell it backwards. Go on, spell it backwards.' I can but not fast like forwards. I have to think a bit after 'a-i-d'.

Mum goes up to do the beds and dusting. Sometimes I help dusting but not today. Today I want to look at the snapshots. I climb on the chair arm and get the tin down from the fireplace cupboard. It's red and gold and there's writing you can feel and trace round with your finger. 'Thoroughgood's Caramels' it says. That makes me want toffee and my mouth goes all watery thinking about sucking that lovely sweetness, pushing the stuck bits off my teeth with the tip of my tongue.

The lid's stiff to open 'cause of rusty bits where it's joined on. It hurts my fingers.

I get all the pictures of me. I spread them out on the table putting the one where I'm smallest at the beginning. Always, in snaps, my head's over to one side. The same side. Now, my hair's long dark ringlets with satin ribbons but in the first picture it's fair and tufts and wispy. Mum said they all kept asking if she put Toddilox on when it got curly and Mum got mad 'cause all she did was brush the curls round her hand.

There's a dog sat next to me as big as I am standing up. My hand's on its head. It's a black dog. Jill. It died. Jill's tongue's over to one side, like my head. But the other side.

This is the very first snap of me. But I'm not a baby that's not even one yet. And I've got fat legs. Not like those thin legs they said about in the hospital. When I had rickets and if my mum and dad hadn't got there in time I had to have irons. So where was I fattened up? There's no pictures of me with little legs. P'raps they looked so sad they didn't want to ever remember them that way.

When I hear Mum shut the bedroom door I put back the tin quick as I can and then there comes tapping. Mum wonders who can be at the front door. That's only for the postman if there's Christmas parcels, or for strangers. This time it's the postman. Tapping on the glass with a penny. He's Sid Dines and Dad said his big flat feet kept him out of the trenches in the war. I wonder how small the trenches were that his feet wouldn't fit in. He's got shiny black shoes. Why do they call shoe-polish 'Cherry Blossom' 'cause that's pink and you don't get pink shoes, only ballet shoes and they don't get polish put on.

'A parcel!' says my mum and writes her name with a little orange pencil on Sid Dines' special notebook where the writing comes out blue on the other side.

'Must be your birthday,' says Sid Dines. He laughs then my mum laughs. I don't know what's funny and Mum doesn't say it's not her birthday not till January. And that's not even this year.

The parcel's square. The string's over double with tight knots and big red blobs of sealing-wax that smells lovely – dusty-barny, warm and candly and the shiny brown paper fresh-polishy.

'Shake it.' Mum's all smiling.

I shake it. It doesn't make any noise.

Mum laughs. 'Just you wait till next time you shake it,' she says.

We're both picking at the knots but they're so tight we have to get the scissors. Mum grumbles at the string being cut 'cause she likes to save all string in the bits-and-bobs drawer. She lets me cut the string. I put the bit with red blobs on in my pocket. I shut my eyes to take the paper off so I can feel what's in the parcel before I look.

It's a little house. It's got knobbly, shiny cream walls, a green door and a red-brown roof with a chimney. There's a slot in the rooftop. Mum says I've got to put all my pennies in: 'They were very good to you – Doctor Barnardo's,' says Mum.

'Dr' it says on the house. I think that means 'Doctor'. I squint up at Mum. 'They', she said. Well I never heard of even one person with such a funny name, never mind two – or three – or four – or... Perhaps these doctors looked after me in the rickets hospital.

'Who are the Doctor Barnardos?'

Doctor Barnardo? He was a very kind man who wanted to help poor little children with no homes and no Mummies and Daddies. He built houses to look after them in.'

'Like this little house?'

'Yes.' Mum gets hold of my hand. 'It's where we got you, duck.'

'From this little house?'

'We-ell… one like this, yes.'

'Did you and Dad come to the house to get me?'

'Well,' says my mum. She goes and gets her purse from the sewing-machine drawer.

I'm thinking very hard. I've got 'didn't want you', 'evacuee', 'chosen' and 'adopted' fitted into a story but now I've got to get this Doctor Barnardo in…

My mum holds out a shilling – 'There you are, my duck, this'll get you off to a good start.'

'Twenty shillings make one pound,' I say. I drop it in slow as I can.

Mum says, 'Now shake it.'

I do twelve shakes – one for each penny of the shilling. I pull over Mum's hand with the purse in and dig out every one of the pennies and ha'pennies and the tiny farthings with the tiny wren on.

'Cheeky!' laughs Mum. But I can see in her eyes she's surprised how hard her little girl's nails are digging into the back of her hand.

Ten more clatters. Then shaking. Thinking and shaking.

Shaking … Shaking … Shaking… Loud.

Louder…! Louder…!! Louder…!!!

'That's enough now, Mavis!' My mum's got her hands over her ears. I pick the box up in both hands and clatter it right next to her face.

'Didn't want you' I shake.

'Adopted' I shake.

'Evacuee' I shake.

'Doctor Barnardo's' I shake.

I shake them loud in my little house. Mum's look-ing right into my face. Mum's not smiling now. She's biting her lip. Looking like crying. Holding out her hand for the box. I can see '*Put it down!*' in her mouth shape.

But her little girl's shaking too hard to hear the words. Her little girl looks away from her and shakes her little house just as hard as she can.

4

Mothers. Late 1946

I won't put any pennies in the Doctor box, I'd thought, but then I do 'cause I want the clattery sound and the shaking and I've got lots of pennies for being good and Auntie-Next-Door gave me a six-pence every Saturday and one day the milkman put a threepenny-bit in. Then, lots of time after – nearly my sixth birthday – I have to have two hands to lift it up and there isn't any clattering so I say what shall we do if it's full? And Mum says about the Doctor Barnardo's lady who'll come and seal it up and take it away to count the money. I feel a bit sad and I say will she bring it back and that's when there's a big banging on the front door and Dad's there but he's not open-ing the door and he's not come back and it's like hammering now.

Then Dad's back but he hasn't opened the door and he's pushed Mum in the kitchen and I can hear his voice gone small and Mum screams. 'No!' Then Dad says some more and Mum comes back.

Her face is white and her eyes like black and she squats down so's her face is near mine and her fingers bruising my arms. She says I mustn't make a sound and do I understand and I nod lots and we tiptoe in the Christmas front-room. Mum lifts me up onto the settee and says I mustn't move. I want to cry but I try to keep nodding.

'Not a sound!'

I nod. I feel my eyes like Mum's now. Big black holes. Like my best doll, Josie, 'cause her eyes fell in-side her head. You can hear them rattle when you pick her up.

The knocking doesn't have any stopping now and I can hear my mum making little trembly- waily sounds and my dad telling her to stay behind and him going along the passage and unlocking the door and that grating over the gravel on the step that sets my teeth on edge.

Next thing I hear is two ladies' voices. One of them's nearly as loud as my dad's but sharp and whiny and then my mum goes out and she's making a sort of crying noise in bits. All the voices get louder and faster and my face is burning hotter and hotter. Then the door slams shut and the voices go like when you're down in the bath and there's water in your ears.

I pull my hands out from under my legs and they're crumpled and tingly then I wriggle to the edge of the settee and get down and tiptoe to the window. I move the pot Springer-spaniel dog and pull back the lace curtain a teeny bit.

There's a tall dark-haired lady holding onto the arm of a short fat lady with grey hair and my mum's clinging onto my dad's arm and she never ever does that and he's waving the other arm towards the ladies and looking mad but like he's got a pain. The dark-haired lady looks nice. Her hair's curly and she's got a sky-blue coat with a little fur collar. I want to see her face but I can only see it a bit from the side. I pull the curtain a little bit more but my mum suddenly jerks her head away from the ladies and I'm frightened she's seen me. I stand back from the window and now the lady in the blue coat's got her back to me. If somebody asked me 'Who's that?' I'd say I didn't know but I feel I do know and I keep looking at her and when she walks away down the steps holding the white iron hand-rail that Dad made, I want to run out so she doesn't go without seeing me but I hurry back to the settee so when Mum comes back in she'll see I've done what I was told and haven't moved. But I'm frightened Mum saw me at the window.

Mum's not coming in here. She's going past the door and into the living-room. She's crying a lot. Dad's talking a bit. Soon I hear her go upstairs and water running in the sink and Dad comes in and gives me one of his treacle toffees and takes me up the garden to sharpen his penknife on the grindstone wheel. He lets me pedal today. It's heavy and wobbly.

When I go back down Mum's there. She puts her arms round me and squeezes till it hurts and says, 'Oh, duck,' and cries a bit again then sniffs and blows her nose and says we'll go and pick some peas for dinner. She must have forgotten I only like those big fat peas in a tin but I nod because what I want to say is, 'Who was that lady in the blue coat?' and I know I can't say that so I go up the garden again and pick peas. I like peas not cooked so I'm trying to put them in my mouth in time with the hatchet coming down where Dad's chopping sticks in the hut.

That was one woman the lady in the blue coat. Who came.

Next morning I didn't go to school. Me and Mum went on holiday to a house with a platform from the house to the lawn where you could put chairs and sit out when it was warm. It was Auntie Jean's house said Mum but I'd never heard of Auntie Jean before. The village where it was had a lovely name - Hanslope – and we stayed there for a whole week and it snowed on the snowdrops and I made a snowman and there was still Christmas cake.

5

'Father: Unstated' (i)

I'd gone down the passage to tap the glass, see if it were set fair for the weekend shooting. There were a letter. It were face-down on the mat – a pale blue square dead-centre, like looking out the little window our Caleb cut in the barn-door. I bent down to pick it up and a bit of the coir mat jagged in under me fingernail like it were a warning summat bad were on the 'orizon. And when I turned it over I knew the 'andwriting straight orff and I'd only seen it the once – when Emmie writ down her address in London for if I got Nance to agree to taking the baby.

'Summat bad' Ye see; that's how I'm always had to talk about her. I reckon as how Nance smelled a rat straight off – allus been good at that she has and you wouldn't get no benefit o' the doubt from Nance – oh, no – even supposing you ever got the chance to put your oar in. Not me, anyroad. Nowt so sure as she'd have got told about me being down street with a gel the last night o' the Fair. She'd have got told that by just about the whole town if you ask me – probably before I even got home. No; the queer thing were, she nivver said nowt – not a dicky bird. Normal, she'd have played me like a fish: bait cast and bobbing, hook swallered and me reeled-in all threshing and gasping on the bank. But this time – when there *were* summat to fish for– nivver a word. Just looks. Them looks of hers. As if I'd crawled out from under a stone – or looks as'd turn me into one. And lots o' the silent treatment – not that that were any turn-up for the books. I couldn't fathom it out. Kept waiting for the axe to fall. Course, wi' what 'appened later I seen there were good reason for the way she were then – as if she knowed it weren't no silly thing and she'd best not push it if she knew which side her bread were buttered.

Then, when I got told about the baby and it were all fixed up for it to be left with Emmie's Mum's mate as she'd been staying with for the Fair, I were frit to death Nance were going to find out everything and we wouldn't have no baby. I expect I were that set on putting her off the scent I went overboard on the nasty stuff I said, as if the worse I called the mother the less it'd 'ave to do with me. And I thought as it'd done the trick.

Until the day we went to get the baby.

When Nance picked her up out the cot she were all cryin' and smilin' and I put me hand on her arm and I said, 'Our little gel.' Nance kissed the baby on the forrid, pulled the pink-for-a-girl shawl she'd knitted tight round her and held her all gathered-in before she turned round and looked me straight in the eye. She weren't smilin' no more and when she spoke it were all slow and quiet.

'My. Little girl.'

That's what she said to me. Not strong-like on the 'my', just the 'our' changed: put right. The tone of her voice were almost, you might say, pleasant.

I knew then. Ice runnin' all down me. I knew what was what.

And she's done a good job wi' 'her little girl'. Oh yes. I'm orff to work afore she's up and I don't see much of her later on by the time I get home, get meself washed up, eat me tea, read the paper. Saturdays I go shootin' or fix guns or gates and cut hedges for folk but I'm fixed a seat on me bike and sometimes I take her in front of me Sundays; go up Caleb's farm or out to old Flackie that's gamekeeper at Pipewell.

Nowt I can say, is there? Never. Ever. It's 'ard sometimes to think I ever 'ad owt to do with it. Mebbe it were all a dream – nightmare, morelike. Folk are allus sayin' my little gel looks just like me – 'Ah, you can tell she's a Pilgrim alright.' – an' I reckon she does but mebbe that's 'cause I want 'er to – to know for sure she's mine. Dunno if she loves 'er old dad – I'm allus bein' told I'm frightenin' 'er wi' me loud voice and me 'obnail boots and whatever. Went on 'oliday with 'em last summer to a Guest House in Llandudno. Last time, said Nance, 'cause I were allus lookin' in gunshops. S'pose I were.

Last time for sex, I missed. Turns out it'd been the time before she found out there were a baby for fosterin' – 'Don't 'ave to go through that mucky business no more,' she said as she signed the forms and pushed 'em over to me. What could I say? She allus hated it anyhow – lying like a plank, head turned away.

Mind, mebbe she dorn't know at all. P'raps it's just once she got the baby she didn't 'ave no more need of me. She's never said owt about 'er looking like me and when anyone else 'as said it she's never said nowt eether way; just 'ad them eyebrows of hers up and a little sneery bit of a smile pullin' up one corner of 'er mouth. Could be just 'er that's jealous and me that's guilty. But other times, them looks go right through you. Then I know all right. Most women – most people – they wouldn't be able to keep quiet about summat big like that. Nance could. Oh, yes. Take it to the grave, Nance will. And I'll 'ave to.

Sometimes I dream of sayin'. Of looking at 'er one day and sayin' – 'You're mine. You're my little gel. I'm your real Daddy.'

The letter were addressed to 'Mr and Mrs'. Damn good job it were me as seen it first – if she'd shown it me out the blue I'd 'ave give the game away and no mistake. Me face went bright red as it were and me heart were stopping then clanging like when the 'ammer's striking the anvil when it starts up again. I were that desperate to rip it open and see what it said but I knew it weren't in my place. Nance is the one as does the readin' and writin' in the 'ouse.

She were in the kitchen peeling tatoes, so as soon as I were able I went through and put the letter on the table. I managed to get out, 'Don't know who that's from,' afore I bolted up the green'ouse to see to the tomatoes. I needed time to go over all the possibilities so as to 'ave some answers. And it'd give Nance the chance to get over the shock – whatever it were – wi'out me there. She wouldn't want me there. Does she ever?

I stayed watering and that about ten minutes wi' me mind goin' round and round. I were tryin' to think mebbe Emmie 'ad changed 'er mind and she'd sign the adoption papers. Anyroad, if it were that, Nance'd have come runnin' up the path waving the letter – an' it were only a few months back Nance 'eard there weren't nothing new on that front. Every year she'd writ and asked the Welfare if they'd got any news but they always said they 'adn't bin able to trace the mother.

Suppose it said she were coming to get 'er little girl back?

When I 'ad that thought I all but blacked out. Me 'ead were all blurry and swimmy wi' the blood rushin' out and I thought I were gunna be sick. Me 'ands were shakin' like an old man's and I couldn't get no stalks tied so I went back down the path, me legs like jelly. What if Nance were there stretched out wi' the shock on the kitchen floor?

I'd allus knew Emmie could easy find out where I lived but the agreement 'ad bin that if I could get the missus to go along wi' taking the baby I wouldn't 'ear no more from 'er. I writ once, end of the first year to ask about adoptin' and I give me work address. It were about three months afore I 'eard back. She just put, 'No. I'm sorry. And I don't live at that address no more.' I knew that were it. And I knew I 'ad to put that out of me mind. And I 'ad to keep it in me head that Nance didn't know.

I went loud across the yard so as she'd 'ear me comin' and then I went in the privy – putting it off. I 'ad to sit on the seat and put me 'ead between me legs and they were skitterin' like a newborn calf's when I went to stand up.

Nance were sitting at the kitchen table, white as a sheet, the letter clutched in 'er hand so's me heart squeezed tight then sank like a ball o' lead.

Her eyes on me. I seen a tiger for the first time last year when we took Mavis on a coach trip to London Zoo. The tiger were be'ind bars. Annie weren't. It weren't just the eyes neether, it were the looking like stone but the same time being all red-hot blood, all ready for the spring – like a bow what's pulled tight afore you let the arrow fly. Them eyes. Hypnotise you, they would. Till I near forgot I weren't s'posed to know who writ the letter nor nothing. I were as near as damnit to asking, 'What does she say?' afore I changed it to, 'Who's the letter from, then?' And I nivver got to say that neether – only the start – 'cause the eyes were riveting me with what they knew – what they'd allus knew – till I 'ad to drop me head and wait. But then I saw that were like an admission o' guilt and I forced me head up and I said, 'Well?'

'Well?' she echoes. And gives a nasty laugh then pushes the piece of blue paper at me. Then she's cryin' – not like the usual waterworks – cryin' so's it'd break your heart. Nothing to be done. She don't want me touching her. I sit down on the chair across from her.

No address. No 'Dear' nothing. Just the one line: 'Coming to see my little girl.'

If she'd put 'daughter': but, 'my little girl' … I knew I were crying but I nivver knew I were whispering – '*Our* little girl. *Our* little girl.' So Nance's heard it afore I'm heard it meself and afore I know it the hand comes out like a whiplash and I'm rocking back on me chair wi' me face stinging. I wouldn't take that, normal.

Then she's got her arms folded and grippin' round her stomach and she's rocking and screaming – screaming 'No! No!' and then, 'Don't you say her name! Don't you say her name!'

I don't know if she means Emmie or the name Emmie give her little girl. But then I realise Nance knows that name – they'd told us in the 'ospital when we got her. So it has to be Emmie she means. But I can't believe she'd care enough about me and her for it to matter whether she knew the name or not. She'd just seemed over the moon she'd got a baby and got the perk of never having to do *that* again. She couldn't 'ave bin jealous. How could she? But ye never know, I s'pose.

23

In a bit she quiets down to weepin', soft, and I get up and put me arm round 'er shoulders and she nivver shakes me orff. I keep sayin' over and over that it's gunna be all right. All right. And that there airnt no way anybody's gettin' to see our little girl.

'She wants to take her away from us,' Nance bawls and I say it don't matter what she wants, she airn't gettin' even a sight of her.

And there's like a cold, hard scoopin' deep in me guts when I think o' poor Emmie and what she might be hoping.

And that's when the knocking on the door comes.

And them two shapes, rippled like, through the glass. Like summat you'd get on the seabed, the silence in your ears like drummin', far orff.

6

Mother

It were horrible. I wish to God I 'adn't never gone there. Worst day of me life, an' that's the God's truth. An' I aint never spoke to me mum since that day. Not that I were in the 'abit of saying much to her anyhow – not since I moved to Southend with Kevin. If it weren't for that barny we had I wouldn't 'ave bin at me ma's an' 'er drippin' 'er poison in me ear. Course, I'm always wondered about my little gel – specially on her birthday – an' hoped she were all right, an' I'd 'ave liked to just see her the once, but things fade. I were that young an' didn't 'ave no money so I 'ad to give up the notion of getting' 'er back one day. Still 'adn't signed 'er away, though. Couldn't quite do that. And then there's Ma sayin' once she were six I wouldn't 'ave no more say 'cause they could legally adopt her. And now, wi' Kevin back and 'im gettin' a job I started to think maybe there were some way I could get her back after all. Then, when I thought of the Mum and Dad I just cried. But still, I wanted to see her.

The house were easy to find. Up on a bank it were: nice; big, an' a little garden just under the window wi' straggly yellow orange and brown flowers, then a rockery bit down the bank an' a little yellowy-colour hedge.The number were twenty-nine, same as me birthday – 'spect I thought that were a good omen, or summat – I dunno what I thought, dunno what I were thinking to go there at all. And with *her*. You'd think I'd have learnt, by my age. There was a white 'andrail, steps up.

First I 'ave to stop an' get be'ind the next door's hedge that's taller 'cause I'm gone all faint an' can't get no breath for climbin' them steps. Ma's tapping 'er toe an' sighing loud an' when she does bother to look at me all she says is, 'Come on gel, me bleedin' feet are killin' me.' There's puffed-up fat all round where the front of her shoe cuts in.

'I feel real bad, Ma.' But she's off up the steps, not bothered if I'm following or not. 'Mum!' I hear my voice, near-crying. She does stop then but she don't turn round. I catch 'er up an' get 'old of 'er arm – hard, round the fat bit, to get 'er be'ind me.

She's teeterin' now an' near falls backwards 'cause them stupid heels are gone off the edge of the step. I get that hot rush an' clench in me middle an' I'm back as a kid, fallin' an her grabbin' me, swearin' an' shakin' me but her face lookin' frightened.

So I'm in front. I have to be, don't I? It's my little gel. I'm the one 'as to speak up, tho' I'm feeling like it's the last thing in the world I can do. But I'm here now. I have to do it.

We're at the top of the steps. That 'andrail's like when they say metal gets so cold yer 'and sticks to it an' the skin gets tore off if yer try to pull it away. But I 'ave to. I 'ave to let go. Have to walk up to the door an' knock.

Nobody comes but I can hear voices inside. Me ma's going on: "Ave a butchers through the letter-box,' an' tryin to elbow me aside. I give 'er a look as shuts even her up. I keep knockin' till I hear foot-steps. I'd scarper now if me knees hadn't gone. I can feel me eyes. Starting out me head an' me heart thumping like it'll burst out me chest. Then I hear the key in the lock.

An old geezer's stood there holding the door be'ind 'im. I can't get a sound out. Me throat's all dried up an' I'd thought it were the granddad. When I recognised 'im I all but died. It don't seem he can speak neither; he just stares. Then me mum gives me a great jab of her elbow and I croak out, 'Hello.'

'She's come to see her,' Ma says. Loud. Nasty. 'She sent a letter.'

He looks at me then. 'She can't.'

I start crying. The one thing I weren't goin' to do. But I can't stop it.

27

There we stand. Me cryin', him lookin' down at the ground, Ma with 'er arms folded. Then Ma says, 'Don't matter. She'll be taking 'er away with 'er soon any'ow. She ain't never signed nothin''

'No!' I try to get it loud but my crying's louder an' I don't think nobody hears. He's got his fists bunched up an' I remember them blacksmith's arms – now I can see it's him. He takes a step towards me mum an' she says, 'I don't bleeding think so, matey,' and he tells us to bugger off back where we come from or he'll get his gun.

I look at him an' his face goes like twisted. I could cry and never stop. I'm stepping back and back.

Me mum's trying another tack, wheedlin' now. 'I've told her. I said: 'Em, yer can 'ardly manage to keep yerself, never mind a kid.' It ain't me as is wanting 'er to take the kid, mister. Way I see it, you make it worth 'er while an' you'll see the back of us…'

Then I'm like wailing: 'No! No! I only want to see her,' but me mum's talking over me an' I hear her say: 'She'll sign alright when she's got five 'undred knicker in her mitt.'

I look straight at him an' I keep on shakin' me head side to side. I know we ain't nothin' to each other but I can't bear it. I can't bear him thinking that about me. Tellin' my little girl that about her mum. It's not that he has to say good things – he don't 'ave to say nothing, except maybe that I did come once. To see what she looked like. To see she were all right. Please God, don't let him tell her I were after money. He won't tell her that, will he? I look for his eyes before I go; look to see in them that he won't tell her that.

I turn back at the top of the steps. And I see her. Just a glance before she ducks down. Dark wavy hair in bunches with lovely blue satin ribbons. Our side's all got fair hair.

Mum's still going on, till he roars an' I reckon he must have give 'er a push 'cause I heard 'er clatterin' back on 'er heels, swearin' blue murder. The last words I'd ever hear her say.

When I got back I packed me stuff an' phoned the garage to tell Kev I were comin' an' we'd stay in Dublin together. Day after I got there I sent off for the adoption papers to sign.

7

'Father: Unstated' (ii)

I went in the hut. When they'd gone. I'd got sticks wanted choppin'. Splittin' a log ye have to grip the hatchet haft strong wi' yer two 'ands when yer liftin' it up above yer head swinging it down. Be knocking yourself out, else. Reckoned that'd stop me hands shakin'. Mind, nivver stopped 'em sweatin'. I were 'aving to wipe the palms on me britches to dry 'em off every few strokes. Still, I'd got a good pile o' sticks an' the lovely smell off of 'em afore Nance come out.

'So that's her.'

She'd said she were stayin' in the 'ouse wi' our Mavis but I cairn't say as I were surprised when she come out at the end. I don't reckon Emmie seen her.

'Must have been under-age. Common as muck!'

My head were down. I said nowt. Started tyin' a bitta twine round some o' the sticks – mek a bundle for by the fire. She smashed the bundle out me hand just as I were doin' the knot.

'Common as muck!'

I nivver looked up at Nance's face but that in 'er voice an' the rage that come up when she hit the sticks down, I knew I were gunna say summat.

'She did *come*. To see her.'

I knew the 'atchet were too heavy for her; mind, she did give it a look afore she got hold of a stick in each hand, holding 'em like daggers so's she could stab all uvver me arms an' trunk. I just stood there. It were good to feel summat in me body; pain in me body. Then she were doing a word with each stab: 'She' *Stab* 'come' *Stab* 'for' *Stab* 'the' *Stab* 'money' *Stab*.

'That were the mother said about the money. Not her.' I said. But she were shakin' her head an' cryin' loud over my words.

Screeching now: 'Lowest of the low. Prostitute. Prostituteprostituteprostituteprostitute …

I put me hand uvver her mouth an' she bit it, hard. I pulled it back an' she stared me down. Then she did like a chant, staring at me wi' boiled-sweet eyes between each bit like I were supposed to repeat it after 'er.

'Tell her. Tell her: 'She were no good. She didn't want you. She came for the money. She were no good.' You tell her that. You keep tellin' her.'

Then she went out the door, looked back uvver 'er shoulder an' said 'I'm taking Mavis to Jean's. You can go down Post Office and send the telegram.

I tried to imagine her saying 'Shall we take Mavis to Jean's?'

'Shall *we*?' That'd be the day! Dorn't know as she's ever said 'Shall we?'

8

Brown-Coat-Woman

There's a woman I'm always seeing down street. She's horrible. She always speaks to me. I don't know why. I don't want her to. If I see her coming in time I always go the other way round, then I'm late for school and get told off. Or late for dinner. And get told off.

She's big and fat with a suet-dumpling face – the shape and the colour. Her hair's stringy on the brown coat she always wears. It's the colour of the school doors' paint and it's so tight round her chest the buttons are pulling out of the buttonholes. Under the brown coat is a brown skirt and grey wavy edges showing under that and if you go down her fat legs her fat feet are bulgy over her shoes that are mucky brown.

Sometimes this woman's got a meanie-eyed boy and a mardy girl trailing behind. That boy's got ringworm circles on his head and his tongue keeps coming out to lick candles that run down from his nose. I can touch my nose with the tip of my tongue. I bet he can't. I never found anybody who can. Only me.

The worst time, Horrible Woman was suddenly at the bottom end of Well Street when I was about a quarter of the way from the top. Like when The Goodie and The Baddie are going to have a shoot-out and everybody in the town goes hiding in their houses – or in the saloon – that's a good word, 'saloon'. We've don't have a saloon in Howell, only pubs.

The monster's coming. Nearer… And nearer… She's ballooning to giant size, making the houses shrink. Fat white legs like maggots, her chest rolling and swelling, the tops of her legs overflowing the buildings each side. Towering. Till there's no light…

I ran and I ran and I ran. And after that day I didn't see Monster Woman again for ages and ages. I nearly forgot all about her. P'raps I imagined her? I do imagine lots of things. 'Imagination'll be the death of her,' they're always saying. But I think imagining's best of all.

That next time I'm going into the butcher's with Mum when MW's coming out. I look away into the window. There's a skinned pig-head dangling from a hook. MW's piggy eyes gleam out from her cheek rounds and the puffed squabby foot-flesh in whitey sling-backs, that's like a pig's trotters.

For the first time ever I feel sick thinking about juicy, sizzling pork sausages. I'm never, ever going to eat them. Never pigs again. Maybe never any animals.

'Hello,' says Mum.

'Nice day,' says MW

I sneak a look at her face. She doesn't really look like a monster today.

She's ducking down towards me: 'Hello, Mavis. How are you, my duck?'

'All right, thank you,' I mumble.

I'm scuffing my sandal toes on the pavement but today Mum doesn't give me the 'Wait-till-I-get-you-home!' look.

We go on a bit. Then I say, 'Who is that woman? She always says 'Hello' to me and I don't like her.'

I get a sharp look but not Mum's usual: 'Not 'woman' – 'lady''

We're beside the Co-op draper's. Mum's gazing in the window like she's seeing rare animals at the zoo instead of old faded boxes and cottons and bits of material. Staring for ages, then when she speaks it's right into the window-glass all small and high-voiced. And she's crushing the bones of my hand till it feels like being caught in Dad's vice.

'That's Mrs Brown.'

I laugh. She crushes harder.

'What are you laughing at?'

'Nothing. Just she's always *brown*. Her brown coat. Everything's brown.'

I have to wait for the next words and they're so squeezed out Mum's lips are hardly apart.

'She … looked after you … a bit … when you first came.'

My blood rushes out of my face and I feel my eyes go wide and black. I'm just staring at my mum.

More words jerk out of my mum's mouth: 'The Welfare Lady took you away … they … found you lying on a sopping mattress …'

'I wet the bed?!'

'No. No. It was her … You wouldn't remember, my duck, you were only a baby.'

Only a baby. But in some way I do seem to remember, so I stare in at the zoo animals too. My fingers have gone numb in my mum's hand. Tears roll down her cheeks and mine.

Monster Woman.

Mrs. Brown.

Looked after me.

When I came.

How did I come? What about Mum and Dad coming to get me from the little house? What's a welfare lady? Where did she take me?

We walk on. Ages and ages.

'Would you like an ice-cream, my duck?'

'Yes please.' You can't talk and lick an ice-cream cone at the same time. We went over the road to Tarry's Ice Cream Parlour. My mum thinks it's common eating ice-cream in the street except at Llandudno on holiday. But today we both get cornets. Sixpenny ones, not threepenny. Big enough to keep us licking all the way home.

Licking my patterns. Trying to fit in the new word: ad-op-ted … e-vac-u-ee … doc-tor bar-nar-dos … *Missussmith*? No. All the rhythm's spoilt. Anyway, it doesn't fit in at all. With all those special words that are about *me*.

Mum's gone to make scones for tea. I'm reading my book. It's *My Friend Flicka* but I'm only pretending to read it 'cause I keep thinking about Mrs Brown, not my friend Flicka. How *could* Mrs Brown have got me? How *could* she? How …? Then there's the slam of the oven door shutting, so the scones are in. I think I'll ask Mum while I'm scraping the leftover scone stuff from round the bowl, so's I can be looking down and it'll take her by surprise and she'll have to answer straight off.

When I open the kitchen door it makes Mum jump but she smiles when I go over to the mixing-bowl and she says we'll have a scone hot out of the oven. While I'm licking the last bit of goo off my middle finger I'm watching my mum 'cause I can see her eyes are getting bigger all the time 'cause she's waiting for the 'Mrs Brown. How?' question.

When the bowl's wiped 'clean as a cat's whisker' Mum clatters it in the sink – yellow stone on yellow stone. The tap gushes out loud so you wouldn't hear if anybody says anything. But she has to turn it off in a minute so I go and stand next to her on my little wooden stool so I'm nearer to her face and I want to ask the 'How?' but … I don't know … it seems such an easy little one-sound word for all the long, hard answer there'd have to be.

I can feel Mum all drawn in, waiting. She's stopped the tap. She's wiping her hands on her apron.

'Where …'

The minute I've said that word and not 'How?' a bit of a smile's coming out on Mum's face.

'… did I go after that?'

Mum's beaming now, close to my face, taking my hands; so glad not to be answering the 'How?'

'That's when you went to the hospital, my duck. You know! You remember.'

Yes. I know. And I know it wasn't Doctor Barnardo at the hospital. Putting ointment on my rickets. And bandages. But I still don't know about them going to get me from the little house. And now there's Mrs Brown that I don't know about.

But I do love the hospital bit of the story. A poor hungry little baby – 'Wah! Wah!' – rescued from the monster's lair and magic-wanded away to the white walls of Kessingham hospital. Made all clean. Soapy bubbles in a baby bath. Swaddled – like baby Jesus – in a big soft white towel. Talcum-powdered. Those nasty old rags pokered into the furnace. Burnt to ashes.

My new beginning.

Between shiny starchy, white hospital-cornered sheets.

9

Mother (ii)

Mrs B. 'Sweet Georgia Brown'. She told me she were called after that song but Ma said rubbish, she were born years before it were writ – and anyway, she weren't called 'Brown' then. Maybe that's why she married Mr Brown. Ma said it were more-like 'cause she were fat, like in the Nursery Rhyme: 'Georgie Porgie Pudding and Pie' She is fat – an' rough an' messy – but there is summat nice about her. Bloody sight sweeter than Ma, any rate. It's just that with her old man buggered-off, an' with three kids of hers an' another she fosters to get a bit extra money she can't cope. Looking at the 'ouse I'm surprised they let her. Must be not many as wants to do it.

It were Ma's big idea – packing me off there. Said it'be a holiday for me, wi' the fair an' that, an' I helped out a bit wi' the kids. Mind, it were really so's she could mess around with her fancy man.

Then there were *him*. Last night o' the fair. Then I didn't get me monthlies. I couldn't believe it. Wouldn't. It were only the once. How's that for luck! So it weren't till after the third miss I had to tell Ma. I don't have to tell you what she said! And she had a mate – Busy Lizzie who was known to 'help girls out.' I said weren't it too late an' the answer I got were a hot bath an' a bottle o' gin. We didn't have a bath but I got sent round to one of her mates as did.

When she could see I were still expecting I said it just hadn't worked. I did sort of have a go but, really, I knew the water weren't hot enough an' I couldn't get down much o' the gin – that's horrible stuff, sorta sweet in a weird way, sickening.

Ma were livid. Said she weren't planning on entering no sodding 'Glamorous Granny' contest yet awhile, thank you very bleeding much. Turns out she's expecting herself.

I were that scared of going to the doctor. Never really had – 'cept for Chickenpox an' that. Stuck-up bastard never even looked at me. Asked a few questions then said he'd write to get me a place in the Home for Unmarried Mothers – said it more like it were 'Filthy Whores.' Needn't 'a worried about him wanting to examine me – it'd 'ave bin beneath him to soil his hands on such as me.

It were horrible. The birth. The baby were the wrong way round – sin punished! It were such a long, long time. Never could I have ever dreamt anything could hurt so much. I screamed that I were tearing in half. Every time I shouted out the nurse would say: 'Stop that now; do you want the doctor to hear you!' an' shake me shoulders, diggin' her fingers in hard. I tried to lift up and see, at the end, but she went, 'No! No!' all hissing and snarling and pushed me back down and she's got her hand over me face – fingers smelling of carbolic soap – I used to love that but I ain't never had it not since that.

They took the baby straight away.

I'm lying there, weak and sore an' cryin' me eyes out. I ask what it is. I ask to see the baby.

The nurse never said nothing but I couldn't bear it an' I grabbed her arm and kept hold till she snapped: 'Girl.'

Then she said 'it' had to go into a special room. To rest.

'You'll have tired the poor thing out with all your carry-on,' she said triumphant-like, snatching her head up. And away she clattered.

I 'spect they took my baby like that 'cause they wanted me to give her away. It's easier if you don't have much to do with them.

I asked to hold her but nobody answered and I was left alone.

I knew I were going to have to leave her there – Ma said I couldn't bring the baby home an' I didn't have no money to take care of her. But I wouldn't sign the papers for adoption. Not yet.

That nurse said I was only thinking about myself and after what I'd done the least I could do was to give 'it' the chance of a decent life with somebody fit to take care of a child.

I knew she were right – the second bit anyway – but I stared her down and never said nothing.

Trust me! Bringing the poor little bugger into the world in wartime. A few months on I got a letter saying as how the kids in the Home were getting evacuated, sent to Northamptonshire where they'd get to be fostered. Except the babies and they'd start off in Kessingham General Hospital.

Kessingham General Hospital! I were staggered, couldn't take it in. Kessingham! That were the town I'd got the train to from St. Pancras on the way to Mrs B. in Howell. Well, first I were smilin' 'cause of that, then next minute I were cryin'. Kessingham were such a long way away. I knew I weren't making sense 'cause I couldn't see her when she were in London but just knowing she were near I always had the feelin' I could if … if I really had to. Or, maybe if I got a lot of money an' then I could take her back an' look after her.

Anyhow, I had to do summat, wi' getting that letter. I borrowed a bit off me mate at work an' I bought a lovely little rose-pink dress wi' frills an' a red satin bow an' I sent it to the Home so's the people she went to would know she had a mum who loved her.

That day I were real pleased wi' meself. But all the days after I were cryin', cryin'.

And me mind were all like tossing. Like there were some thought as were pushin' to get out. I couldn't lose that feelin'. Then, days later I knew what the thought were soon as I woke up:

Mrs Brown. Mrs Brown weren't far off from Kessingham. And Mrs Brown did the fosterin'. She could get in touch with the hospital, say she were best friends with the baby's Gran – summat like that.

I could go an' see her.

I near lost all me breath wi' the excitement of it.

I could go an' see her.

The thought had come into me head just like any ordinary, thought, like the thousands that come in every day. But then, when I'd got the thought out an' spoke it, it were like a big weight rolling toward me an' pushin' me an' me reeling back hardly able to get me breath, all tight in me chest an' cryin' again.

I could go an' see her.

It happened.

It did happen.

It all happened

Mrs Brown got my baby.

They must have been that desperate what with the war comin' and all them extra kids, they couldn't have asked too many questions. Only too glad to get rid of one – especially as people weren't so keen on the kids from Homes – specially not babies.

An' it were a near thing that I'd written at all. I never knew if Mrs B could read an' write an' I didn't want to get her mad, showing her up. But I did write. And she did go to the Welfare and they did get in touch with the hospital. An' it were all a miracle.

Now all I had to do were get some hours in the paper shop as well as the Cockney tavern so's I could get the price of a train ticket.

To go and see her.

To go and see my little gel.

More cryin'. So many tears. But for happiness this time.

I writ an' said I were comin' but I never heard nothing, so I just got my ticket an' went. Mrs B weren't goin' to be far away, were she? Not in Howell. It weren't like London. God knows! Nice though – knowin' everybody – I s'pose.

So, like I said, I were prepared for them not bein' in, but I'd never thought o' nothin' worse than that. But it *were* worse. Much, much worse.

My baby weren't there.

I felt all the blood drain out me face an' I had to sit down. Mrs B. said she hadn't got no letter but I reckon she were just hoping I wouldn't come if I never heard back. Or hanging on trying to think of an excuse for my baby not bein' there.

She went over by the sink an' her face were all red an' she were clatterin' about in the sink with her back to me. I got hold of her arm, hard, and pulled so's she had to turn round but then she's lookin' down at the flags, goin' on about the Welfare woman coming 'cause the hospital wanted all the kids back.

Then she said somebody were goin' to adopt my baby but I shouted an' shouted that that couldn't be true, couldn't be true 'cause I hadn't never signed nothing.

Her gel come in then an' said, 'That's right, it were last week, 'cause the bed were wet an' the baby were allus cryin' an' they said our mam weren't looking after her proper.'

Her mam hit her round the head then an' I were runnin' out doubled-over as if I'd bin punched in the guts.

My baby. My poor little gel. Poor little mite. Left there wet an' cold. Cryin' an' cryin'. How could she? How could she?

I went down Well Lane 'cause I couldn't let nobody see me an' be askin' what were up. I sat on a wall till I could stop cryin' enough to get meself to the bus stop. I felt sick wi' wantin' to get out of that place.

Wantin' to be at the hospital in Kessingham. I'd worked out if I were lucky wi' the bus I'd have an hour to sort things out before the train went. I weren't leavin' till I'd got it sorted never mind the train. There'd be another, or I'd kip down on the platform.

Mind, even afore I'd got off the bus I knew it were no good. A young gel turns up at the hospital sayin' she's the baby's mum? Wi' no papers nor nothing? Even if I had stuff they wouldn't let me near her. Like when she were born.

I wouldn't even be able to pick her out.

That thought made me bend over an' grip round my body. I thought I were fallin' apart.

Wouldn't be able to pick her out.

It like stabbed me; but after, I had a really weird feeling, Near like being' glad. Glad I were feelin' so bad 'cause, after the first few days, gradually it had got so's I weren't feeling much. It were hard to believe I'd got a baby at all, wi' not seein' her – not even as she come out of me. Not seein' her get born – that should make anyone cry and never stop.

Me mate, Pauline, they made her feed the baby an' everythin'. That were cruel but she said it were 'cause she were lettin' him be adopted – so's she'd be quite sure. Even if her heart were broke. Thinking about her I'd felt such guilt – what were wrong wi' me? Hadn't I got no heart to break?

'Wouldn't know my own baby.' The words that made me know I'd got a heart, all right.

Wouldn't know its father either. Not in the daylight… In Fair lights. In moonlight.

I tried to picture him. Dark wavy hair, brown eyes, strong arms –blacksmith's arms. Blacksmith. My breath stops. Shod horses in the War. Now he works in Kessingham foundry. He must be here now. I could … what? It's his child as well. But he don't even know. What if I tell him? He told me how much his wife wanted a baby an' how maybe it were his fault an' things might have bin different if there were a baby…

And now there is a baby. Here. A baby. Waiting in the hospital for a Mum and Dad.

My heart were thumping, all sense in me saying 'Stop this!' But I couldn't. I wouldn't. This were my only chance.

I asked for the foundry. It were five minutes along the road. When I got there I stood just round a corner. I could hear the iron banging, see the sparks flying, feel the heat. I were feelin' sick an' me legs were wobbly. I couldn't do it. But I couldn't seem to move neither.

Then I pushed meself off the wall an' I were walking forward, like a robot. There were a man bending an' banging some lump of iron with a great hammer – he seen me an' stopped what he were doing. He asked were I looking for someone an' I said no. Then I said yes, I were looking for William. He said he'd go an' fetch him 'cause he were on the anvil an' wouldn't hear. He went in where the sparks were shooting out from an' a man come out wi' overalls on an' shoving up his goggles. He seen me an' looked puzzled an' stopped, so I said, 'It's me,' an' he come forward an' then he seen who it were – he were all black from the fire an' that but even a couple of yards back you could see him go white under it. He half turned then an' I thought he were going back in. I weren't going to stop him – reckon I'd have been glad. But he never, he come on an' we went out the gates an' round the corner so's you could hear yourself speak.

He said, 'Emmie?' like he thought I might be a ghost an' I nodded an' I were pleased he remembered me name an' I said I had summat to ask him an' I'd forgot for a minute he didn't even know about the baby.

I told him. He had to hold on some railings an' when I said he had a little girl his face all twisted up an' he cried a bit.

When I saw that I knew he cared an' I got me courage up and told him my plan an' first he shook his head then he looked at me more hard an' said how did he know it were his baby an' I said *I* knew it were an' he could only take my word for it. Then I said, anyhow, if they'd been adopting a baby they wouldn't know anything about whose baby it were. He were quiet for a bit after that and then I said I'd have to get the last train an' he said he'd have to think about it all.

I give him my address an' he touched my hair. I left him still clinging on the railings. I nearly turned round an' said, 'You can buy her a bunch of red balloons,' but I never. I thought he'd have forgot. About the red balloon he caught for me. On the Noah's Ark.

10

'Father: Unstated'

I can't hardly think about that day she come. Nobody ever come there. Not to nobody's workplace. Not for me, nor nobody. Never had. So that were the first thing. Then, when I seen her, well, first I couldn't mek it out – some young gel stood there. I were look- ing at her, frowning I reckon, with her starting to look frit. Then she said 'It's me,' an' I knew, but some'ow I couldn't know. An' me legs were shaking an' like in- side me an' all. It were like it were a ghost – no, not that, not ghost 'cause what she were to me were like somethin' in a fairytale. But it *were* like it weren't real an' I damned near turned round an' went back in the forge. If she hadn't made a move wi' her hand … so that I seen her shoulders like drooped down an' her mouth goin' an' knowing mine would too if I kept stood there. So I managed to get some sorta words out an' I led her off out the yard away from the clatter so's to hear ourselves speak. That's when it hit me – there were a girl an' she were wi' *me*. It were Emmie. The only woman I'd had in me arms in more'n twenty years.

Then she's telling me.

A baby.

Mine.

My baby.

My little girl.

I've give a woman a baby! I can't speak. I'm crying. And I'm thinking I have to give my baby something. You always give a present when a baby comes. What will I give her – my little girl?

Then the Howell voices are coming in: 'Wur, ye great soft bugger, 'ow d'ye know it's yours? Your got no way a' knowing. Believe owt, you would. Nothing in all them years wi' Nance an' now yer believing some young gel as turns up from London an' says it's yours. After one quickie! Yer dorn't know who she is. Wouldn't even a' picked her out in the street., knows a soft touch when she sees one, she does all right. Oh, yes!'

When she says I'll have to tek her word for it I'm the father I ask her if the baby looks like me. Turns out they nivver let her see it. I'm got me hands shoved in me pockets then an' looking down at the ground, to keep from crying and taking her in me arms. Poor girl, poor Emmie. I ask her why she's telling me now when she didn't afore. Seems wi' me being married an' so far away she weren't meaning to trouble me. Then when there were the evacuation an' the fostering plan went wrong she's in Kessingham an' remembers I work 'ere an' that I'd said about not being able to have no children and – looking up at me so piteous now, them tears pricking me again.

Well, first I wanted to roar an' shout an' push her away an' run. Then all me body went heavy and I were looking in her eyes an' … I dunno'. It were such a mix of feelings. I said I'd think about what she'd said an' she give me her address. Inside I were tickled pink about it. Maybe I could mek up some story an' get Nance to come round to it. I reckoned I could. Reckoned I could.

I were smiling that much when I went back in the forge an' I got a wink an' a punch against me shoulder from Anvil, as we call 'im. It were a daze, the rest o' the day. Wonder I kept goin' at all.

11

1947 Loganberry Drupelets and Other Roundnesses

I'm old enough to go visiting on my own now. Best is going to see my aunt Zilla. She's my dad's sister. But they don't speak. So I used to just see her sometimes down street when I was with my mum. Then a little while ago she said I could go for my tea and Mum said that was nice and I did and when we made the bed she showed me hospital corners.

'My Aunt Zilla does hospital corners,' I bragged to Pretty Rosie when she said she helped her mum make the bed.

'You haven't got an aunt Zilla.'

'Yes I have.'

'That's a stupid name – Zilla. And who wants to sweep corners in a hospital, anyway?'

I laugh 'cause I think she's making a joke but she's not. Pretty Rosie's stupid and nor will she admit she wants me to show her how to do hospital corners either.

Mine aren't very good yet but Aunt Zilla does them in two shakes of a lamb's tail. She helped a long time at the Cottage Hospital when she was fourteen and she wanted to train to be a nurse there when she left school but it closed down when they built the big hospital in Kessingham. That one where they got me. Now Aunt Zilla works with Aunt Beat in the box factory doing corners on *boxes*, not sheets. I can do those too. I love the white shiny smell of the paper.

My dad goes to work. My mum makes lattice tarts. Every two weeks. Always Mondays in the autumn 'cause the blackberries get picked on Sunday 'cause Dad's not at work and not out shooting pheasants or rabbits or pigeons and he's got his blackberry-hook so's we can get all the big fat juicy ones that are always up high with lots of nasty, sharp prickles round them. 'Come on, I'll 'ave yer, yer buggers.' Dad says. And he does. Auntie Lewis-next-door saw him with the hook then he had to make her one. And he made her a wooden thing for getting your wellies off by the door.

It's loganberries me and Aunt Zilla are picking today. They're lovely – like big, long more-pink raspberries with giant round bits. Aunt Zilla's face is smiling at me through the criss-cross canes and there's all berries and viny leaves decorating round so her face looks white and her eyes black liquidy. She's in a frame – like a picture. I say that, and Aunt Zilla says 'Lattice'. Oh, that's why it's 'lattice tart!' I'd always thought it was like apple-tart. But it was silly thinking that 'cause it can be blackberries – or raspberries – or loganberries. Or it could be cherries – or plums. And they'd all be lattice tart. But 'lattice' sounds all delicate and lacy – nothing like hot, sugary, fruity tart.

It's hot, picking. We go and sit under the apple tree and eat some of the berries. I'm licking the juice off my fingers and fanning them out in the dew grass then I see the scylla leaves. I ask Aunt Zilla if scyllas were named after her.

She smiles. 'I think scyllas came first, sweetie pie.'

'So *you* were named after scyllas – when they saw your bright blue eyes.'

Aunt Zilla says she's sure that was the way of it, even if some boring people have the notion of 'Zilla' being short for 'Priscilla'.

When Aunt Zilla goes in to get orange squash and yellow cake I start off down the lawn to see what butterfly that is fluttering round the wallflowers. Then I stop 'cause there's somebody in the deckchair. My eyebrows pull together. It's 'Uncle' Ecta. He's so horrible and my auntie's so lovely I don't know why he's there with his bum bulging the canvas so it's like a big ball and all the stripes wonky and his head a shiny white ball up the other end and his giant round belly up and down up and down and the watch-chain on it like a silvery slithering snake. His lizardy eyes are shut. I hate him.

I go back where I was to see how many head-over-heels I can do before Aunt Zilla gets back. There's room for six each way.

'… seventeen … eighteen …' I'm getting faster, my crêpe soles turning like the seats on the Big Wheel. I'm getting out of puff. I'm glad to hear the glasses jingling on the tin tray. I stop turning and sit up.

'Uncle' Ecta's not asleep any more, not lying in the deckchair. 'Uncle' Ecta's standing up and he's staring at me. His tortoise neck's jutted forward and he's looking all funny so it makes me go bright red and scramble up quick as I can and push down my skirt.

It gets really really hot and Pretty Rosie's prinking around in shorts with her brown legs. 'Can I wear shorts, Mum? Please?'

Mum says I haven't got any shorts and why would she be spending good money on shorts when I've got lovely frocks she's made for me.

Pretty Rosie's mum doesn't make her frocks. But her auntie in America sent her some *trousers*. Red ones.

In Howell girls don't wear trousers – only Brenda West with her army camouflage ones and her hair so short there's bristles all up her neck and you wouldn't want to touch it. I said to Mum about her voice like a man and Mum said it was because she smoked 60 Woodbines a day: 'Funny gel. Never had a boyfriend nor nothing.'

Mind there is a snap of me with pull-ups when I was three. It's black-and-white but Mum said they were pink pull-ups. I remember they were itchy.

Trousers would be good on this wall. My arms are fatter 'cause of the heat and the satin-binding round the sleeves of my mum-made frock pinches and my knees are getting red circles where I have to grip the rough bit. It's a good wall though for riding with the bricks on top curved over so it makes like a saddle.

Sometimes I have to give little kicks with my heels to spur on my steed. Then I get thin white scratches on my new Clarks sandals – they're chestnut colour like conkers and so's my horse. I'm thinking I'll have to lick my finger and rub in some dirt but after a bit I can see there's red sandy dust coming off the wall in puffs. That'll colour in the scratches.

There's a hot, toasty smell from the bricks all mixed up with the white smell of my crêpe soles. I've got my eyes closed, sniffing to get all the smell I can till my tongue starts curling and aching.

Then I hear it: 'Mmm!'

Who's that? There's somebody here. I squint against the sun. I think I see Aunt Zilla's face. I'm just going to call when I look harder. Oh. Her face is down on the grass. And 'Uncle' Ecta's face is there too. Just above hers. I think he's hurting her. He's got to let her go. Why doesn't she scream? I hate him. My hands go all bunched up. I'll hit him and hit him and hit him …

Then comes Aunt Zilla's voice: 'Ecta. Stop! There's somebody there.'

I should shout 'It's me, Auntie.' I should run to help. But I'm biting my lip and it's bleeding and my stomach hurts so much I only want to run and run and hide.

Now Ecta's telling Aunt Zilla not to be daft 'cause Rupe's gone cattle market, the kid's in the 'ouse and there airnt no bugger else. He's telling Aunt Zilla to have a bit of sense and to get her skirt up. I know that's not having a bit of sense. That's bad. And I see my auntie's head jerk away from him and her eyes are like the cows' when the men are prodding them up the ramp when they're going to be killed and the cows know. I'm not going to the cattle market again – I told Dad but he just laughed. But I won't go. I won't. Next time I'll scream and scream and tie myself onto something.

Aunt Zilla's seen me now. She pushing him hard with two hands and putting her knee up. I can see her hating him on her face. He doesn't see it 'cause he's too busy scrabbling to his feet. Ooh, I wish, I wish he'd seen her hating. I wish he had.

He's coming over. He's got his arms stretched out: 'Wanna get down, then? Come on me duck.'

I'm not his duck. I hate him. I'll kill him.

Before I can move he's got his warty, sweaty, meaty hands under my white knickers and he's lifting me down. 'Ha!' he goes so there's a cloud of mutton-fat, pickled onions and baccy comes out of his mouth. The inside of the tops of my legs are all scraped and stinging but still I hold on and a great loud fart comes from Ecta in his struggle to get me off the wall.

Aunt Zilla heard the fart. Her face is all crumpled rose-petal like when tears make that sort of achy bruisy knot under the bone of your cheeks before spilling out. I'm glad they're not spilling out of Aunt Zilla's eyes. I won't know what to do. There's shining, but grown-ups can blink tears back in better.

Hand-in-hand me and Aunt Zilla walk away from the brickyard up the lane, over the fields and over the stream. Usually we do Troll and Great Big Billy Goat Gruff on the bridge and jump till the plank bounces up and down and makes creaky noises and we squeal 'cause we might fall in. But we don't today.

At the top of the hill we get to the witchy-fingers' tree that doesn't get leaves and is all sooty-black with a great big hole at its middle where you can stand in except there's beetly wormy things. The tree was struck by lightning. 'Uncle' Ecta could be struck by lightning. I could say a spell at the witchy-tree for 'Uncle' Ecta to be struck by lightning.

'Who is 'Uncle' Ecta?' I say. It comes out very small.

Aunt Zilla doesn't seem to have any voice. Her mouth opens but nothing comes out for ages and then a whispering: 'Uncle Ecta …'

I wait but there isn't any more.

Aunt Zilla's sister lives with her. She's Aunt Beat and they live in Underwood Road. It's not under a wood but there are two little trees that get white flowers and then red berries after. 'Mountain Ash,' says Aunt Beat; 'Rowan,' says Aunt Zilla and sings out loudly: 'Oh, the oak and the ash and the bonnie rowan tree, they flourish for me in my ain country.'

There's a giant plant in the window. Aunt Beat watches everything from behind it and from up close outside you can see the leaves go down her face like the bars of a cage. The plant's in that war-song my dad sings: 'The Biggest Aspidistra in the World.'

It's all brown in their living-room. The teapot's shiny brown on the furry brown caterpillar tablecloth and it's a got a light brown and dark brown knitted cosy like a ploughed field. And there's Aunt Beat – her hair, her eyes, her dress, her cardi, her stockings, her shoes. All some sort of brown. And dark brown hair, oval shape so she looks like a flea.

When we go in she doesn't move. And we don't move. Only the pendulum of the Grandfather clock moves – it swings from side to side, ticking 'You're late! You're late!'

I don't know if anybody will ever speak again but then Aunt Beat does – in a sneery voice: 'Brought His Lordship's washing, then?'

She hasn't turned round to look at us so she must have been watching us come up the street. I was thinking that bundle Aunt Zilla had was a giant suet pudding. Aunt Zilla doesn't answer about the washing but she bangs out of the room, wrenches open the under-stairs door, kicks the suet pudding in as hard as she can, slams the door on it, comes back in, grabs hold of the teapot and swings it up as high as her head. It looks like she's going to smash it on the floor but she doesn't, she just slams it down again on its stand so some tea splashes out. I think 'Good thing the cloth's brown,' but I don't say it.

And that's when Aunt Beat does turn round. She gets up, lifts the teapot and sets it down very firmly in the exact centre of the table. I think she must have measured it and made a mark only she can see. She pours a cup of tea. No steam's coming up and it looks like when there's oil in a rain puddle. She pushes it over to Aunt Zilla and some slops out in the saucer.

She looks at me her lips all stretched out to look like a kind smiley auntie and says, 'Are you going to have a cup of tea with your old auntie this week, me duck?' She asks me this every week. I've never ever had a cup of tea, so why does she keep asking me? I want to ask her that but you can't say 'Why?' to a grown-up. That's cheeky. And 'cheeky' is one of my mum's worst things. I'm just about to say the usual 'No, thank you,' nicely, when there's a big roar from

Aunt Zilla: 'Tea? What tea? Where's the tea? Call this tea?' Every bit she says she gets louder.

I'm a bit frightened now and holding my breath in. Not a sound out of Aunt Beat though, just a twisty smile and her eyebrows up nearly in her hair. She looks at the clock that's at quarter past four and says all calm: 'At four o'clock I called it tea.'

I know what she means but I just get a picture of Aunt Beat standing to attention when the clock chimes then pointing a witchy finger at the "Four' and saying 'Tea!'

A laugh comes out. Just a bit. But enough for Aunt Zilla to hear and she's glaring at me, her lips pressed so tight her chin's all crumpetty. Then she stomps out to the kitchen and we can hear the tea sloshing down the sink and the cup banging down on the saucer. Aunt Beat's looking at me with her mouth like a zip. Then the corners turn up a small bit and she goes to get the oak biscuit barrel. She does every-thing slow – making out the lid's stuck, going round and round the rim with her claw fingers to ease it off. I pretend to myself I'm waiting with her because that's polite but I do really want that ginger biscuit. Then I have to say 'Thank you' extra nicely and look at her and smile to make up for going straight outside with my biscuit. Then she slams the lid back on hard as she can and I can feel her beetle-black eyes boring between my shoulder bones. And I know she's mad 'cause I'm going after Aunt Zilla. But she'll be glad the crumbs'll be in the garden and not on the mat.

Aunt Zilla's crouched down pulling groundsel so hard it looks like she might topple over backwards –

p'raps she's imagining it's Aunt Beat's hair! I go and stand next to her and I want to tell her about thinking of Aunt Beat calling it tea 'cause I know she'd find it funny. But then, if she laughed she'd be admitting she'd been jealous and grown-ups didn't do that. Not to children. Not even Aunt Zilla who wasn't anything like other grown-ups.

When I kick a big clump of soil it smells lovely and earthy and all mixed in with the polish and leather and crêpe from my sandals. Aunt Zilla's sitting back on her heels now, looking at the soil under her finger-nails. Then she turns her head, swings her arm towards me and says, 'Come on, sweetheart, give us a hand up,' and I'm so happy I could cry.

I'll never ever laugh at anything Aunt Beat says again. And I'll never ask things like: 'Who *is* 'Uncle' Ecta?'

12

1949. Death at the Box Factory

This morning I went to the Box Factory to see Aunt Zilla. I always do on Saturdays. I love the Box Factory and I love Aunt Zilla and I always run and skip all the way down so I'm going fast as I can but I make sure not to step on the witchy cracks. Then at the end I hold hard onto the wall corner that you can swing round to get everything in your eyes all at once like turning over the next snapshot quick.

Da-Daa…! It's the best ever today 'cause the way the sun is, the red bricks are a wall of fire, the hot colour of the furnace-mouth at the foundry when my dad pulls the little door open with the poker thing. Blazing and your hands going up to cover your face and I nearly do that this morning as if I'm feeling the flame-tongues trying to lick me and this is only a wall.

So for a bit I'm dazzled but then I can see a white shape on the top windowsill that looks like the sea-anemone in my *Life in the Deep Ocean* book. After I squint a bit, frondy fingery bits are waving about like when the sea-anemone's getting ready to attack its prey. I don't even get time to blink when all the body shoots forward like from a catapult and makes my heart bang really fast. And then I see one of the bricks is moving and there are sandy puffs round it. First it's falling like in slow-motion at the pictures and I think I can make it stop if I concentrate hard enough but then it goes so fast like a guillotine and that's when I see the skinned-pig lardy-pink head of 'Uncle' Ecta. And I see the ring of gingery hair that makes it a perfect target.

Nothing's moving now and not any sound and my head's turning all black and empty inside.

I keep my eyes squeezed closed and make my favourite Box Factory pictures come. The great big windmill we saw when we went to the seaside. It had steep twisty Box Factory stairs my mum was too fat and puffing to get up. She said it was the old dust made her puff. And the clack-clack sound the sails made was like the boxes'-paper being pushed out the mouth-slot of the dark-green-shiny machine and the white paper like the clouds through the sky-circle at the top of the windmill and the rustlings like the wind coming over the cornfield the windmill stood in. And there's big piles of rough yellow board with bits of straw in that smell lovely and Aunt Zilla pops me up to sit on them and she calls them 'bales' – like after harvesting – and they smell like them but a bit older. And the best smell's the glue that gets in the holes behind your nose and you feel twitches all in there and down your tongue and round your eyes and you want to just pull it in more and more till you go dizzy and more dizzy with Aunt Zilla and Aunt Beat's long scissor-hands flying and the paper streaming.

I wish now I hadn't thought of Aunt Zilla's hands. I'm seeing that white windowsill sea-anemone. That's like a hand. The knob bits down my back are hurting from the wall so I let go the corner and my hand's all white and blood-beads along my heart-line like Pretty Rosie's beads that she says are real rubies but they're not. And that's just with *holding* a brick. Not pushing it out of a wall!

So I'm standing there shaking when I hear Aunt Zilla: 'These old bricks!' she says and Aunt Beat says 'Ah, well, s'pose they're getting' on, same as we all are.'

They can't see me but I can see them.

I can see Aunt Zilla stepping back from the window and Aunt Beat's hen neck stretched out and her hairgrip-lips snapping shut.

But I can't see 'Uncle' Ecta's head.

Of course I can't see 'Uncle' Ecta's head. Because it isn't there! Where it is, is in *my* head. It's 'Imagination'll be the death of you!' time again. Headlines Ha! *Head*lines – *Uncle' Ecta Dies Today. Bullseye!*

I laugh. Then I feel a bit bad 'cause I do hate his head and I did say I hate him and in Sunday School they said you're not supposed to hate anybody. Jesus loves us all and we have to try and be like Jesus. When I say my prayers tonight I'll say 'Forgive us our trespasses. And being cruel about 'Uncle' Ecta and his head'… And his other bulgy bits!

It's brawn for dinner. 'Pig's head,' says Dad. I laugh and Mum glares at him and says '*Brawn*.' She runs a knife round inside, upends the bowl, bangs the bottom and out it slithers with a horrible sucking sound. It sits on the plate looking like a weird bald head and when Mum digs the spoon in it quivers like a monster jellyfish.

'I don't want any,' I say and Mum says 'See! You've put the child off, you and your big mouth.'

At four o'clock there's a tapping on the window, it's the milkman come for his money; he's the only one who taps on the window.

'Why can't he knock on the bloody door like any other bugger,' says my dad.

'Ssh! He'll hear you,' says Mum.

The milkman's name's Alfie Curtis but I always thought it was 'Curds' and that made me laugh, with him being a milkman and Little Miss Muffet eating her curds and whey. And I thought his horse Queenie was 'Creamy' cos it is that colour – like the curds.

My dad wants to go on at him about him tapping the window but he daren't so he says '*You're* late to-day,' instead.

'And I bet you'd like to know why I'm late today,' says Alfie Curtis and pushes his check cap up on his head and goggles his bulls-eye eyes.

Mum looks at him, widens her own eyes and says 'We-ell?' as if she's dying to know. Dad says 'I don't doubt you're going to tell us.'

Alfie Curtis keeps his face turned to Mum. 'I'm had to stop an' wait till the ambulance had done its business, haven't I.'

We're all listening now and Mum says, 'An ambulance?' We've rarely seen an ambulance in Rowell.

'Yep,' says Alfie Curtis and stops.

'Oh, dear,' says Mum and Dad says, 'Well? D'you know as who were in this ambulance?'

'I do an' all,' says Alfie Curtis and we wait some more.

My dad grunts, crosses one leg over the other and goes back to his *Exchange and Mart.*

'It were that bloke from down brickyard.'

'Rupe?' says Dad.

'No. The other one.'

'Not Ecta?' says Mum. 'Is he all right?'

'All right? He's dead.'

It's like I've been punched in the stomach. When I'd run off from the Box Factory I'd gone and sat in the Rec so's I'd get home at the usual time and I was thinking about Rapunzel in the tower and the witch at the bottom and how it was just a story and so was what I'd made up about the brick and 'Uncle' Ecta and what I'm like – how if I see a coal-sack or something on the road I always think it's a dog or cat run over and how that day I thought that church lily in the cricket field hedge was a dead hand sticking up and how I never kick a paper bag because of that story where a head's cut off and turns up everywhere upside-down and grinning so my toes curl like a woodlouse when I think of the feel of it against them. It's no wonder I'm seeing heads at the bottom of walls.

But Alfie Curtis is saying 'Uncle' Ecta's really dead.

'He weren't that old,' my dad's saying, 'only a few years older than me.'

'He's younger,' says my mum – '*was*. Oh dear. Oh dear. Poor Zilla.'

My dad snorts at this. 'D'you know 'ow it 'appened? Heart attack or summat?'

'They reckon that were it. Them two old biddies as work at the Box Factory found 'im lyin' outside when they come out of work. Stone dead 'e were.'

Brick dead, I think and go red with horror. And shame.

'Oh dear,' says my Mum, 'our Mavis were down Box Factory earlier. Thank God she didn't see nothing. Fancy that! Ecta Norton.

I think maybe I'll faint. Gill Sumpter fainted in Assembly. 'Stand up, stand up for Jesus,' we were singing and she went *down*. So I could feel laughing bubbling in my tummy even tho' I felt sick from the thud when she slapped down on the wooden floor. I told Pretty Rosie and she said *she* fainted in church but she didn't. Anyway she's only been to church about once.

'Well, best be off,' says Alfie Curtis, 'I'm all be'ind like the back of a pantomime horse.' He laughs, showing large yellow teeth.

'Are you all right our Mavis?' says Mum and I go more and more red like a beetroot and I have to say something to make her not guess so I say, 'I'm sad,' and I make my bottom lip go pully and shaky. (Forgive me Jesus for telling lies too.)

Dad stares at me as if I've gone mad but my mum glares at him and snaps, 'Of course the child's upset. He should have had more sense than to come out with it like that in front of her.'

I sniff a bit and creep off into the other room. I get on the prickly settee with my book open so they'll think I've 'got my bloody head stuck in a book as usual', but I'm thinking. I'm thinking hard.

'Uncle' Ecta's dead. That's true.

'Uncle' Ecta was dead outside the Box Factory. That's true.

Aunt Beat and Aunt Zilla found him. That's true.

There was something on the brick and the brick fell down. That's true.

I saw 'Uncle' Ecta under the window. Well, I thought so. But I must have imagined it.

Even if I did see him – even with the brick – he could have just died. Without the brick hitting. That's true.

If 'Uncle' Ecta was there and he was under the brick and the brick hit him by accident. Yes. That's possible.

It could have been an accident. That's true ... Aunt Zilla hears footsteps. They don't come up the stairs. She's puzzled and goes to look out the window. By accident she knocks a brick out. 'Uncle' Ecta's lying dead underneath so even if she pushed a million, trillion bricks and they all fell on his head it wouldn't matter because you can't murder somebody who's already dead. That's true.

It could have been an accident.

Why didn't I go and see? See if he was all right. Shout for help ... Help him ...

I was frightened... only for a minute though. Until I knew it was just me imagining seeing 'Uncle' Ecta there. Yes. Of course! How silly! I go to the Box Factory every Saturday and I don't ever remember seeing 'Uncle' Ecta there. I don't even know if he ever goes there. I only imagined him there today because I'd got that thing about his head.

But I do really wish I hadn't said about his horrible head and about hating him and I do really wish he hadn't died today even with his horrible head.

Dad went to the funeral. Mum asked him if he spoke to Aunt Beat or Aunt Zilla and he said that no he didn't and she said you'd think you'd speak to your sisters. At a funeral! I asked Dad if there were crows and he said 'Allus crows at a cemetery.'

Aunt Zilla's frightened of crows. When they build their nests in the big old elm tree behind the Box Factory they come swooping backwards and forwards carrying twigs and Aunt Zilla goes running dodging across the yard with her arms crossed over head. She calls crows 'funeral gloves'.

I wanted to ask Dad how Aunt Zilla looked when the gravedigger shovelled the earth onto the coffin. When the clods hit the wood did she think about the brick hitting the head that was under that lid? Did she feel that she'd be sucked under by giant white worms as a punishment?

It's all horrible.

I hate round things.

I remember when I didn't even notice round things.

I remember sunny days. And skipping.

I remember before Mum and Dad talked to me in the Christmas-only-front-room.

It's all horrible now. And Dad brought the Funeral Service paper from the church and it said the funeral was for *Hector.*

No! It must be a mistake. I know about Hector – I read the story of Hector The Hero. 'He Who Holds Fast' in my *Greek Heroes* book.

Uncle *Ecta.* Hector. Uncle Ecta is – *was* – Uncle Hector. But I bet none of them has even heard of Hector the Noble Son of Priam.

How I hate them here. Why can't they speak properly? It doesn't matter mostly, but you'd think the least they could do would be to get people's names right.

That's two of my books spoilt today. When I grow up I won't speak like people here.

13

Mavis Spherophobic

Today Pretty Rosie's coming for tea. I don't like Rosie very much but she's my age and they think she looks 'nice' and she lives just over the road so they call her 'Mavis's friend Rosie'. She's got long blonde plaits like Rapunzel and *Rapunzel*'s my favourite story from when my teacher Mrs. Campion told it and I don't think it's fair that it's Rosie looks like her and not me. Rosie only reads comics. I'm not allowed comics except I used to get a Rupert book at Christmas.

Rosie's got her orange squash in my Little Grey Squirrel cup and her eyes are going all round over the rim and she whispers – 'I squeezed my titties in a cup and milk came out.' She nods her silly shiny head three times 'cause she can see I don't believe her. '*Yes,*' she says loud and hissy and pulling her face all grown-up serious and wagging her head up and down again.

'No it didn't. And anyway you shouldn't say 'titties'. It's horrible.

She chokes a bit on her orange squash and my face is going hot and I know she didn't get milk but my chest gets sort of itchy and prickly so I want to rub it hard with my fists and smooth it down flat.

'You've got to go now,' I tell Pretty Rosie. 'Mum says.'

She looks surprised but doesn't argue.

When she gets to the door she swishes her plaits and turns round and mouths over her shoulder – 'It di-id!'

That was yesterday. Me and Dad are going up to the farm on our bikes this morning like we do on Sundays when Dad's not shooting.

When we get near there's new-splashed cow-pats and they make my toes curl up so I have to lift my feet off the pedals and they go whizzing round like pinwheels and I take one hand off to pinch my nose shut.

'Get yer 'ands on them 'andlebars!' Dad's bellowing but he's a good twenty cowpats behind and can't catch me so I take the other hand off as well.

'Way up, Mavis' – that's Uncle Caleb from the cowshed. He's my dad's and Aunt Zilla and Aunt Beat's brother – 'the baby of the family' they call him but that's silly 'cause he's big and old. Mind, he's got no hair, like a baby.

'Wanna give me a hand with the milking?'

I did one time. Disgusting swinging pink udders with cow-dirt smeared all over so I couldn't drink milk for ages. I shake my head.

I'm off to see the chicks. Chicks are clean. And fluffy. Primrose yellow with dry neat little feet that tickle the palm of your hand. Chicks haven't got any messy hanging bits. Chicks peck dry grain and make tiny droppings.

I prop my bike against the railings between the lawn and the hen-run where lots of Berberis grows in summer, the mass of yellow so bright against the black-green yew tree. The strong scent from it fills up your nose and mouth so you can't smell cows and milk any more.

In the hen-run a few brown speckled hens and a couple of Banty roosters are scratching and scurrying, clucking and flapping. No chicks. They're probably in the warm of the kitchen.

I follow the crunchy gravel round to the farmhouse door that's propped open with a milk-churn. Over by the yellowy stone sink there's a great dollop of sour milk set on a three-legged stool to drip through butter muslin into a big earth pot all crusted. The cade lamb's skittering all over the red flagstones and butting at the stool to bring it down and get the milk. 'Baa-aa' it goes when it sees me and I pat it and shoo it outside. I can feel the stone cold through my sandals and it smells sour in there.'

'Is that you, Mavis?'

That's Ruth, my cousin, John's wife. She's nice, she's from Kessingham and she's very tall and got wild red frizzy hair. When I go through to the parlour she's sitting in the armchair, she says the chicks are by the range where it's warmer for them. I can hear their thin cheeping coming from the cardboard box. I go over and Ruth says can I bring the white towel from off the pulley and when I take it I see what she's doing and I go hot and red. 'Oh', I say, and 'Sorry.'

'Don't be silly,' smiles Ruth and takes my hand and my fingers go all stiff and she puts them on the baby's head and says, 'Feel his hair,' in a hushed way and I do and it's softer than anything in the world, softer than the chicks, like thistledown and there's a big sweet feeling coming at the back of my throat and my fingers are getting soft but then the finger I'm stroking with suddenly slopes down into a hollow and it jerks back as if I'd touched the stove. I look down and see a dip in the baby's head with something beating under the skin.

Ruth laughs: 'It's all right, all newborn babies have that; it's called the fontanelle, it soon closes up. She smiles and I'm just beginning to breathe properly again when the tiny creature stirs from its milky sleepiness and becomes unfixed. Ruth clucks like a mother hen. I clear my throat and try to say I'm going in the front room but the words won't come out. I try to look away but I can't. I catch Ruth's eye, then her hair makes me think of Medusa the Gorgon so I'm 'transfixed in horror' like Perseus was in my book. Now the baby's face has gone that dark-red colour my mum calls 'puce' and it's all creased with furrows like in a ploughed field. Then its worm-slimy-pink mouth goes square to cry and it's like a black cave with a grub waggling about at the bottom. And now there's another round thing – 'sphere', that's the word: it's milk-white, twice the size of the baby's head and stretched to bursting with blue veins Medusa-snaking across it and a flat browny disc with something like the valve I screw my bike-pump on sticking up in the middle, all puckered. Then suddenly it's gone, sucked-in by that guzzling mouth.

The small sphere is devouring the bigger one! Like that picture of a snake eating a baby crocodile. I think I might be sick.

My head's gone to cotton-wool. I can't hear the chicks any more … I might faint.

'Come and help me change him,' invites Ruth from a long way off. She snaps open and eases out the giant safety-pins on either side, holds her baby's puffs of ankles together with thumb and first two fingers of one hand and tweaks the damp towelling from beneath his tiny bottom with the other. I see a lumpy plum-shaped sac, the shrivelled skin angry-red as a turkey wattle, a spout jutting from it that peters-out in crumpling.

'There we are,' announces Ruth and swings her small clean son up to her face to receive the adoration of her smacking kiss. 'Look at his fingernails, like those tiny tellin shells we got at the seaside last year. Would you like to hold him?'

14

May Day Party 1950

No. I do not want to hold the baby.

Not Ruth's baby.

Not any baby.

Not ever.

It's not fair. I was caught off-guard. My cousin's always been lovely, frizzy-red-haired, pail-clattering, seed-scattering, clucking Ruth. With a Land-Armyjumpered chest. Now it's all spoilt. I've seen what's underneath. I'll never get it out of my mind – that bulging pink-whiteness, those awful sucking sounds.

I couldn't wait to get home to my mum. *She* doesn't have any truck with bosoms, breasts, bristols, knockers or titties. My mum's got a 'bust'. Her top half is reined-in by whalebone, decently camouflaged by layers of vest, brassière, petticoat, frock and cardigan. There's no hint even of two segments, never mind browny-red bits sticking out from them.

But there's more to come – to 'loom large' as it says in books.

It's Hothwell Junior School's May Day Party. That sounds lovely, doesn't it? And I specially love 'May Day' – the words rhyming, the way they make me think of hedges white with May blossom, and specially, of the poem my mum recites every year: 'For I'm to be Queen of the May, mother, I'm to be Queen of the May …'

So I'm happy, putting on my blue satin party frock and the matching hair bows. Off I go, my hand in my dad's, trotting along beside him. Of course, I'm not so silly as to be expecting the May Queen's 'maddest, merriest day' but I *am* feeling excited.

Until we get to the school door. It's wide open – 'Welcome Everybody!' And everybody's in there. Shouting. And laughing. *I* want to shout. *I* want to laugh. But inside I've gone like full of cold suet pudding and I can't see and hear properly – all I get is pictures of those times when I tried shouting and laughing. Picturing *them*. Looking sideways at each other, turning their backs on me. Hearing them. Their big sighs and groans, their sniggers.

'I don't want to go. I don't want to go.' My voice is wobbling and I'm pulling back against my dad's hand.

'Dorn't be so silly.'

'I'm not. I feel sick. I really do, Dad'

'You'll be all right once you get in.'

'No. Please, Dad. I don't want to …'

My fingers are gripping as tight as they can go but of course my dad has no trouble letting go my hand. He gives me a bit of a push between my shoulder-blades and I'm in. He'd say it's 'being cruel to be kind' so all I can do is blink fast as I can to try and keep the tears back.

It's like I'm in a glass box. And all round this box my schoolmates are *Round-Things-On-Stalks* and the 'round things' keep splitting open and spurts of noise come out. On each side of the main stalk there's a thinner stalk ending in a twiggy bit and from some of the twiggy bits a thread goes up straight like a snake-charmer's snake. I follow it up and see it blossom into a beautiful red balloon. I love balloons. In my head I float up to them. Free. Out of everybody's reach. In another sphere.

The peace doesn't last long. A great clattering breaks out below me and the *Round-Things-On-Stalks* are elbowing and jostling, trying to get sat as near as they can to whatever it is that's been carried in and set down as the centrepiece on a round red-crêpe-paper-covered table.

'Make way! Make way!' cries one of the teachers in her special 'jolly' May-Day voice as she staggers under the weight of a leaning tower of white pudding dishes. The *Round-Things-On-Stalks* part on either side of her so I get a bird's-eye view of the 'crock of gold' on the table – it's a monster moulded breast-shaped milky thing and it wobbles and quivers. Ugh! Bl'mange. Bl'mange is my pet hate. After brawn. (Imagine – you could have pig's-head first then blanc-mange for dessert!)

Just when I'm thinking this the blancmange-bearing lady straightens up. There's a long pin holding on her pheasant-feathered hat. It catches and punctures one of the hovering balloons. Bang! In that one instant the beautiful thing shrivels into a shred of grubby-blue rubber with blubbery fish-lips at the end. The stupid *Round-Things-On-Stalks* fall about laughing, clapping and cheering. Pheasant-Hat blows a whistle then threatens that they'll get no jelly, trifle or blancmange till they've polished off every crumb of the soggy sandwiched triangles of fish-paste, or meat-paste.

In between sandwiches and jelly it's announced that Musical Chairs and Pass-the-Orange-Under-The-Chin will be played.

I'm out of here! With Musical Chairs I'll just be first one out so that's ok. But, Pass-the-Orange-Under-the-Chin! *That* is a *team* game! First I won't get chosen so I'll have to stand there trying to look as if I don't care when the Rosies and Judys prink off leaving '*that Mavis*' to be glared at and mumbled onto the end of the team that's drawn the short straw. Then there'll be the 'Go *on*!!' screamings, the head-clutching, the groans as the orange somehow escapes my desperately thrusting chin and 'my' team comes last.

No. I'll go and wait it out in the caretaker's hut till I reckon it's time for the silver-paper-wrapped chocolate Swiss rolls. I love those. I'm planning to eat two – at least – to make up for not having had my ration of glutinous jelly and lumpy blancmange.

In the hut there's old desks you can sit at with lids that are all inked-in carvings. There's a few full names but mostly initials, some of them at the ends of Cupid arrows that have pierced through hearts. Do you put your beloved's initials on the tip end or the feather end? Same difference. These lucky ones have all been chosen. There's five 'so-and-so loves JB' but no trace of JB loving anybody. Imagine being JB! Or any of the chosen ones, come to that.

'Being chosen' is right at the top of my list. I read that story where a man gives his soul to the devil. Well, the devil would be welcome to my soul if only I could, just once, hear my name called on the team – or be chosen as monitor – or for a part in the school play – or bearing the Boar's Head in hand – or carrying the teacher's books – or doing bus-duty – or anything. I don't know anybody else as bad as me – who cares about this as much as me. P'raps it was all that 'We chose you' stuff I used to get when I was little? Whatever. It's like having toothache in every bit of my body – there's the longing mixed with the knowing that, given half a chance I could amaze everybody.

Why don't they see it? The ball slips out of my hands because *they* expect it to and *I* know they expect it to.

I wait till it goes eating-quiet then I creep back in. I'm looking round wondering where to sit when somebody calls out my name. It's the new girl in my class, she's waving with one hand and she's got the other on the seat of the chair next to her. She's kept it for me. For *me*! She's *chosen me!* There's a great glowing inside me and it's tears of joy I'm blinking back now. I'm putting on my paper hat. I'm laughing. And eating. Just like everyone else! 'Wowee!'

It seems only minutes before all that's left of the May Day feast is blobs of red white and pink frogspawn and crumbs floating in lemonade pools. Now it's time for cards from the Special May Day post-box (it's the Special Christmas post-box really, they've just pasted over the red crêpe with flowery paper. Do they paste a new layer each year – with the box getting bigger every time?)

I never get a May Day card so I pretend to be busy folding a paper napkin into something.

'Mavis!'

What?! That was my name! The teacher said 'Mavis'. There's such a great rainbow-bubble of joy forming and getting bigger and bigger in my chest that I think I might die before I ever get to the Special May Day Box. I'm dream-walking … dream-walking … then, there's a sudden movement over to my right and I slow down. There's another girl coming to the May Day Box. She's coming faster than me. She's in front of me. She …

Mrs Hetherington – the doctor's wife and School Governor – has seen her now. She's frowning at the envelope in her hand, touching the sleeve of Mr. Evans the Headmaster. He puts his fingers over hers then goes red. He mumbles something then says to the other girl and to me – 'Wait a minute, girls. We'll have to open it.' He takes hold of the envelope, slides the card out and reads out, 'Love from Jean', and …

'That's my friend,' the other Mavis says loudly and she's stepped forward with her hand out.

I stay back. The wise grown-ups will be bound to sort it out.

'Is that right, Jean?' Mr Evans calls across.

The other Mavis glares at Jean. And Jean – my one friend in school – Jean, nods her head and makes little giggly sniggery noises.

I'm struck dumb. But still I'm sure the right thing will happen. Everybody knows Jean's *my* friend and they know that other Mavis isn't even in the same class, and doesn't live anywhere near us – *and* she's 'common.'

But the right thing doesn't happen. The other Mavis snatches the card, doesn't even say 'Thank you' and stumps back to her place, staring me down with bold black eyes..

Why? Why would she do that? Why would she want a card meant for somebody else? I'm scalded inside as if the rainbow bubble burst and it was full of acid. And somehow I've got to get back to my seat.

When I do, I look across at Jean. Her face is turned away and it's all streaky red. I can see she's upset at what she did and I can see too that, even more, she's scared of the other Mavis. I stare hard at the sidepiece of Jean's round flesh-pink-rimmed glasses held on with grubby flesh-pink sticking plaster. They've slipped down lopsided from the bridge of her nose because of her fright-sweat. I want to smash them into her stupid round blinking red-rimmed hen-eyes. Then I can't see any more because of the tears but when Mrs Hetherington looks over I have to pull up my mouth and smile and smile till the muscles under my cheekbones go all achy.

I've folded one of the red serviettes four times to make a square. If you folded it forty times it'd go up to the moon; if you folded it fifty times it'd go up to the sun and if you folded it ninety-four times it'd go as high as the whole universe. I read about it in my encyclopaedia; it's called 'exponential growth'. But you can only fold a piece of paper six times. Nobody ever believes that. But it's true. *You* try it and you'll see. Now I'll do a green triangle and dip the point in that puddle of squash and count 'one-elephant' 'two-elephant' … to see how long it'll take for … Oh. They're all clapping. The cards are done.

Now it's 'Prizes for Good Work'. My name's called for a Composition prize but it doesn't really make up for anything – the prize is for my work, not for *me*.

But when I tear the brown-paper wrapping off the book I'm so thrilled I forget all that. It's *Grimm's Fairy Tales*! It must be especially for me – Mrs Campion must have said to them. There's a crying-lump down in my throat when I stroke my finger over the narrow ridges running from top to bottom on the dark-honey colour of the cover with carved hearts in-set between. And in the centre there's a circle and in the circle there's a boy and he's wearing elf-shoes, sit-ting cross-legged, guarded on each side by a huge fierce black cat with amber eye-slits.

It feels like opening my gold-edged Bible, a soft rustle and my first finger going trembly trying to turn over the page so's I don't pull it and make it tear. Oh, you should see the lining inside the cover; it's dark blue-marbled – that's like the patterns on marbles – with the edge of every page sky blue. And the fron-tispiece is a coloured picture from 'Hansel and Gretel' – 'Suddenly the door opened and an old woman lean-ing on a crutch hobbled out (Page 15)' it says in blue letters underneath.

In my head I say 'Rapunzel, Rapunzel, let down your hair; that I may climb without a stair' and it's just like an 'Open Sesame', the book opens right at the first page of my favourite story. When our teacher, Mrs Campion read it to us she always showed us the picture with the prince climbing the 'magnificent long hair like spun gold' and all round him were sharp thorns like the witch's pointy teeth and nose and nails and chin. Mrs Campion made us say 'Charles Folkard' five times while we were looking at the picture and then she'd close the book and a few minutes later she'd say 'And *who* painted that picture?'

'Charles Folkard, Miss,' somebody would answer.

'Charles Folkard, what?!'

And we'd all chorus: 'Charles Folkard, Mrs Campion.'

I'm so happy I want to run home fast as I can but I don't. I walk so carefully with my hands crossed over my treasure, guarding it close to my heart. Next thing I know there's a push in my back and I go flying and me and my book are together in the gutter. Blood wells up on my knees and trickles down but that isn't what makes me cry; it's seeing the spine of my poor book all twisted and broken and its pages fluttering white on the tarmac like a butterfly hit by a car.

A boy with snot-candles and grey hand-me-down trousers kept up with string goes to kick at the book; he doesn't have a sock on the kicking foot, and there aren't any laces in the boot.

His big brother pushes him out of the way and says, 'No. Let's take it.'

'Yeah,' says their big sister and steps out of the Fire Station doorway with her hands in her pockets. She comes slowly forwards, looking at me then she picks up the book. She keeps looking at me while she rips out a page and crumples it up and drops it. Then she grinds it into the tarmac round and round with the heel of her Wellie.

It is that girl. The girl who took my card. The *other* Mavis.

When I'm watching them run off down the street the girl's second name comes to me – it's 'Brown'. They're Mrs Brown's children. I knew I'd seen that girl somewhere outside of school. So maybe they didn't just happen to pick on me – maybe their mum had told them it was my fault she got into trouble and I got taken away from her.

And – if I hadn't got taken away that girl would have been my sort-of sister and those boys … That's when I start crying.

My hands and knees are all studded with grit and bleeding and stinging. I go limping along School Lane and all I can think of is my poor book and those Jack-o'-Lantern faces jeering at me. Then, when I get to where School Lane runs into High Street I see my book. It's thrown face-down in the gutter.

I can't bear to tell my mum anything, so before I go in I hide my book between two stones in the rockery. When I go in I get stingy iodine and a bandage and go upstairs to bed on stiff sore knees. So, so sore.

Next morning I get the book and put it in a brown paper bag in my bedroom drawer under my vests and knickers and ankle socks – all the pure white things.

15

Knowing Blue

All white things. And me feeling like one of them when I wake up the next morning.

White and washed-out and blurry as if I haven't slept a wink tho' I don't remember being awake. From downstairs comes the roar and bump of Mum's Hoover and, from the back-yard, the clang of dad hammering some horse-shoe or gun-part or whatever.

I have to get out.

I'll go down Fanny Joyce's Lane – it's my favourite place after the Box Factory and I haven't been there so much since the brick day. Mum said Aunt Zilla asked her why when they met down street and mum said she thought I'd been upset about 'Uncle' Ecta. Like she knew the stuff I'd been imagining! But she couldn't. It was just the first thing that came into her mind.

Several times I've asked older people who Fanny Joyce was but they'll never say – they all claimed they didn't know.

'Fanny Joyce…?' They'd wrinkle up their foreheads, purse their mouths, shake their heads and say, 'Cairn't rightly remember.'

That's stupid. If you were asking about someone who'd done them down a hundred years ago they'd remember alright! Yet they make out they've forgotten someone so important that part of the town had been named after her. Hm! They just don't want to tell me for some reason. And if they really don't remember I don't think much of them either way.

One time my mum told me about seeing a man and a woman down Fanny Joyce's lane 'doing things'. I remember thinking the woman must have been Fanny Joyce. That wasn't like my mum, talking about anything like that and her voice kept going all stumbly and sort of dragged down. It made me think it was how she'd felt watching them that did that – and then I thought how my mum would have a fit if she knew I was thinking that because the whole point of her telling me was supposed to be a warning, to show me how wicked and evil these things were that the man and woman did and how disgusted my mum had been. I did know that mostly she'd feel disgusted because more than once she'd boasted, about my dad: 'Never laid a finger on me, he didn't. Not after we got you.' and tho' I only half knew and didn't want to know what she was telling me, I had understood – and I'd been horrified my mum would say that to me. You didn't tell your little girl that sort of thing. Not the being proud of it. And anyway it was private.

In my mum's Fanny Joyce's tale she was out with Dad for an evening stroll when, just before the second stile, they heard a rustling in the long grass by the hedge. Mum had said 'Ssh!' and put her hand on Dad's arm to stay him. It might be a rabbit, she'd thought – she liked seeing a rabbit run across the field, its white scut bobbing. Next thing the hedge parsley was all swaying and they'd heard a laugh – like when you've got your hand over your mouth. Mum had been rooted to the spot 'cause she knew it was a couple…

I looked at her, wanting to cry. I didn't want to hear any more. Mum saw my face then and looked like *she* wanted to cry. Then she said, nearly whispering, 'I thought your dad was going to shout out…' And her voice quavered to a stop.

Today The Lane's all lace with Hedge Parsley, and with the sun on it, it smells of lace as well – old, going-yellow lace soaked in sun and heavy from the dust of all the years it's been hanging there. If you look close up at one head of the Hedge Parsley you'll see it's like a parasol a bride carries, with green spokes. I wonder if Fanny Joyce was ever a bride.

By the first stile there's a sycamore, its leaves that pure, light green of the beginning of summer. In spring it put out pink saplings, the thickness of my thumb. They looked like baby ostrich legs; especially as the leaves were soft and uncurled as they burst out of the bud like a sprouting of downy feathers.

The hum of insects mingled with the heavy scent of the honeysuckle makes my head spin. Lovely. I take in great gulps of it and the gunge in my head that I woke up with this morning begins to melt away. It's like when you duck down with a towel over your head above a bowl of camphorated oil cubes in boiling water.

Over the stile there's Totty Grass nodding its thousands of goldy- bronze heads and there's a goldfinch. It arrows down and perches on a clump of ragwort, singing and swaying. You feel you can see the yellows from the ragwort and the goldfinch brushing off on each other.

Next is the bluebell coppice. This is where I had my 'blue thing' last spring. I'd been lying on my back, eyes closed so it was like drowning in the flowers' deep-blue scent. And when I opened them I was pierced by blueness. It went into my skin like an injection. It filled all the spaces inside me.

I. KNEW. BLUE.

Blue.

And I knew it had been given to me, somehow, this magical 'knowing blue'.

Today, I stretch out among the flowers and the grass stalks. I say 'Ouch!' when I try to straighten my sore knees but I soon forget them because down here you can hear the breeze in the Totty Grass. It's like shingle shifting and settling as the little waves creep back to the sea. My eyelids are beginning to droop when something strange happens: there's some way a sudden bright patch and a swaying grass-stalk come together so that one of the Totty Grass heads looms; it looms to about a hundred times its actual size. It's frightening. It's grotesque. I blink and blink and blink to get it back in focus but it's like it's imprinted on my eyes. And now I see it for what it is. Oh, God! It's a bald head! Bald – except for a ring of russet hair. Bald! Except for a ring of russet hair! Like … Oh, God! No-ooo…! No-ooo!

I'm up and running as fast as my legs will carry me, sore knees forgotten. The breeze has grown suddenly icy-cold. I'm running and running and being sure not to let myself look down at the bad-luck goblin-green fairy rings.

By the time I get to the lane I'm gasping and I've got a stitch in my side. I need to sit on the seat to get my breath back. Years ago I used to sit on this seat collecting car numbers. Not that I knew anything at all about car-registration, I just liked writing the numbers down all neat in rows in my special little red notebook that said 'Car Numbers' on the front and had a cigarette-card of an Austin Seven that I'd stuck underneath that.

Well, what with feeling all muzzy this morning and the sun and my sore knees I haven't been on the seat five minutes before I begin to get that lovely heavy feeling that means you're going to fall asleep. I don't think I've ever had that in the daytime before, except when I'm in bed, ill. That's only old people. But it is a lovely feeling…

And that's the last thought I remember.

I don't know where I am when I wake up and I think I've been awoken by a cloud covering the sun, making my skin colder and my eyelids open because the day's not bright like it was. I blink, I yawn, I stretch and then I find out what's shading the sun from me. My elbow nudges something. Something warm! I jump in shock. I sit up and yank my arm back in.

There is somebody on the seat with me!

I sneak a sideways look. It's Sammy the Sweep. Dumb Sammy.

'My mother said that I never should, Play with the gypsies in the Wood.' My mother said 'Don't you speak to Sammy the Sweep.'

I feel my heart miss a beat. Sammy the Sweep! A Gypsy in the wood! What should I do? Pretty Rosie said he was a Dirty Old Man and I said it was just the chimney soot and Rosie said, 'Stupid!' She didn't mean that sort of 'dirty'. I pushed her, for whatever it was she did mean and I shouted: 'You don't know. You don't know anything.' And Rosie said everybody knew – that was why he couldn't talk – because he was a Dirty Old Man: 'It's a punishment. He's been struck dumb.' 'I wish you were,' I said.

Just in case, though, I've pulled both my elbows in and I'm checking my skirt's down over my knees, 'cause you have to do that, to be decent, if there's a man around. When I'd pulled in the arm that touched Sammy the Sweep my hand caught on a bit of the seat-wood and now there's was a splinter right in under the skin of my palm. I tip my hand a bit to see, just looking down with my eyes, not moving my head in case Sammy the Sweep sees. The splinter's a really fine one, nothing sticking out to get hold of. It'll be a rough needle and tweezers job for sure if my dad sees it. I can feel Sammy the Sweep looking at me. His look's pushing at the side of my face and I don't know what to do. When I was little doing the car numbers I could've just jumped down off the seat and run away. What's that they say about dogs that are going to attack you? Is it 'Look them in the eyes?' – or '*Don't* look them in the eyes'?

I try turning and giving Sammy the Sweep a half-look, in case I've got the wrong one. He smiles. Just a small smile. Then he looks down at the hand where the splinter is. He moves his hand towards me as if he's going to get hold of mine. 'Scream now,' I think. But somehow I don't. I let Sammy the Sweep take my hand. I let him turn it over. He brings it up a bit nearer his eyes, takes a good look and then points to the sky with his other hand.

I look – high. I can see an aeroplane, tiny because it's almost out of sight. Sammy the Sweep holds my splinter-hand up high and then I see. I see what's the same about the plane and the splinter: they're both stitched; one into the blue, the other into the skin of my palm. I smile. It's a wonderful thing.

And I look straight into the eyes of Sammy the Sweep. I see they are very blue. Blue eyes. Blue sky. Blue. I know he can't speak so I suppose he can't hear but I just have to say it – 'I know blue,' is what I say.

'Yes,' says Sammy. And smiles.

Going on along the road, out of habit, I start the chant: 'My mother said' … then I stop. I change it to making up a 'blue' poem for Sammy. Much as I want to triumph over Pretty Rosie, I shall never tell her or anyone Sammy can speak. And he knows I won't. It's our secret. No-one else deserves to know. Maybe Sammy the Sweep has his reasons for being dumb.

16

Mavis is Seen to Bloom

The summer I'm thirteen it's a scorcher. 'RECORD HEATWAVE' proclaims the Kessingham *Evening Telegraph*. Everybody's cheering at this headline and there's me thinking 'Oh, no!'– Me; who loves the sun more than anyone! All weekend and every day after school there they all are splashing about in Howell Swimming Pool at the bottom of the Rec. I'd give my right arm to go too but there's no way I'm being seen in that bathing-costume. (*Bathing* costume! Everybody 'cept my mum calls it *swimming* costume – and it's *swimsuit* in Girls' Crystal.)

Whatever. The bathing-costume. Is bright orange. And – wait for it – is wool. A bathing-costume. Knitted. From orange wool.

Orange.

And wool.

Orange wool??

I hate it so much just the thought of it brings tears to my eyes. I beg and beg and beg for a ruched nylon swimming-costume but my mum says there's still plenty of wear in the one I've got. *Wear!* That's the whole point – I won't wear it. *Can't* wear it.

'But ....'

'I said "No"'.

'But, Mu -um ...'

'Leave it, Mavis.'

Crying doesn't work either.

It just gets hotter and hotter. It gets to 89 degrees Fahrenheit! I give in. I fumble in my drawer and my mouth feels drawn like when you suck a lemon. My fingers jerk back when they touch the itchy, loathsome orange wool – Ugh! I can feel it in the back of my throat. I have to yank at the wretched thing to get it out – the leg-hole's got stuck on something – it would, wouldn't it! It's a sign. An omen. I shouldn't go. 'Don't go, Mavis. Don't go!' But I want to go! Everybody else is there. I want to go! I can hear the heavenly splashing. I can feel it. And it's so, so hot.

I go.

The back of the changing-cubicle's corrugated iron, so you've got to mind the rusty jaggy bits so you don't get lockjaw and die like Brenda Willis up Glen Hill last summer when she got a pitchfork in her foot, haymaking. I'd been playing with her up the farm the day before. It was so sad. I heard them say I was in shock. I didn't know children could die – not somebody I knew. She was always there at the farm then one day she wasn't. Not ever again. So now I always pull on my costume facing in to the iron so I won't catch myself on it by accident.

I'm just bending down to pick up my sandals when I freeze, like you do when you're playing 'Statues'. Somebody's made a hole in the corrugated iron. It's perfectly round and it's bunged up with something. Something that looks like a brown-and-white marble. Then it moves. It's an eye. The white's all bulging like a cow's in the slaughter-house. I stop breathing. I'm nailed to the spot, shivering. I pull up the orange wool and clutch it against me. I can feel my eyes are nearly as wide as the Peeping Tom's. Then the eye goes still. A dead man's eye. I can hear myself making little breathy, mewling sounds.

A boy's voice says 'Psst! Come 'ere. Come an' look 'ere. This one's got summat!'

Keeping hold of the top of my costume with one hand I scrabble like a mad thing at the cubicle door till I manage to get out onto the slimy concrete at the edge of the pool. I keep my back to the shouting pool and my fingers are trembling so much I can hardly manage to tie the bow but when I do at last it's so tight round my neck it's crippling and I have a job to lift my head. I jump straight in and do a big, splashy crawl to get away as fast as I can. But with every stroke I can feel the wool getting more sodden and more heavy, so it's dragging the costume down from my chest. I'm in between choking and sobbing and I don't want to ever get out of the water but in the end I get so tired and cold that I have to. When I do I look down and I see the Peeping Tom had been right – I have got 'summat' – not much, but definitely something. Something that I didn't have before.

I scramble out of the horrible-smelling water and I'm clinging onto my top with both hands – out of shame, not modesty.

I have bloomed. Like a rose? When it's not possible for anyone to observe the change from bud to flower? No. More like a mushroom: white domes that push up sudden from the night earth.

On the sideboard stands a framed photo of me on my first day at Kessingham High School for Girls. I pick this up and I study it. The blazer's new and stiff and there's a badge on the pocket that says 'Members One of Another'. The blazer's buttoned-up over the gymslip that's got box pleats. All is straight as a die.

So, nothing was sprouting back then. But – just like with a fungus – there'd been a hidden growing underneath the warm layers of dark winter's woollies.

When I look at the class summer photo I see the regulation stripes are bent out of line where they cross the area of my – 'developing' – as they call it. Tears fill my eyes. Nobody else I know has this. Why me?

All I can think of is getting a bra. I beg for a bra. Day after day. On and on. But all I get from my mum is 'Silly!' and how I'm still just her little girl.

This is not how the tradesmen of the town see it:

'Geddin' ter be a big gel,' leers the butcher, with a livid, slippery ox-heart in his meaty paws, eyes ogling my chest.

'Geddin' ter be a big gel,' leers the baker, kneading the hot flour rolls in his basket, eyes ogling my chest.

'Geddin' ter be a big gel,' leers the greengrocer, weighing a melon on his palm, eyes ogling my chest.

'Geddin' ter be a big gel,' leer the butcher, the baker, the candlestick-maker.

And – 'Yes,' – smiles my mum to all of these, with pride in the growth her feeding-up has brought about – 'She'll be taller than me afore much longer.'

'Aaagh!' Why can't she see it? I am in despair. I do keep on – even more – about the bra but I can't bring myself to say about the butcher and everybody. What I can do is to wear a buttoned-to-the neck woollen navy-blue cardigan through the hottest English summer since records began, often dangerously close to passing out, sweat trickling in small rivulets down my burning face.

'Why don't you take off your cardigan if you're hot?' people say.

'No. No. I'm okay. I'm not that hot. I'll take it off if I get too hot. I'm okay.'

But they don't see the third-degree heat rash on the upper half of my body.

I usually dread freezing chilblained winter. But this year how I long for its coverings. And by the time autumn comes the lines of the new term's gymslip are straying very noticeably from the vertical. Something has to happen before the stripes of summer come round again. Drastic measures are called for.

I'm in the bathroom. My feet are lapped by loops of curdled-cream crêpe bandage. I'm looking down in panic. I can't step out – the circle's enchanted. I shake my head to get rid of such fanciful nonsense and I bend to pick up the bandage. It's lukewarm from my body heat and damp from my sweat. Revolting! My fingers let go involuntarily and my feet jerk back but, too late; a coil manages to tighten round my ankle and the length of it slithers across the lino after me like a sloughed-off snakeskin. Kicking wildly to get rid of the thing leaves me face-on to the mirror. And *that* stops me in my tracks!

Not only has my bosom-binding failed to shrink anything but it's given me twin hummocks that look as if they've been criss-crossed by the rolling tracks of a snow-plough. And, to cap it all, thanks to a cunning flaw in the cheap mirror-glass my right breast is a squabbed-out sphere gashed by the rubbery smile of a toothless old crone.

'Mirror, mirror on the wall …'

Sobbing with rage and despair I wrench the mirror off the wall and smash it with all the force I can down onto the edge of the bath.

Mother will go mad. There'll be seven years' bad luck. Smithereens of it.

But this is not what happens! Not even seven months. And in fact, it's on Friday the thirteenth of the next May (the 13 not mentioned to Mum!) that I get my longed-for bra.

Who's superstitious?

The magic purchase is to be made at Hothwell Co-op Drapery.

I'm in seventh heaven. I'm moving so fast my mum's way behind puffing and complaining, but wild horses couldn't hold me back. When we get to the glassed door of the Co-op Drapery I see that crook-backed Mr Lee from upstairs in Furnishings is downstairs in Lingerie, stretched on tiptoe, fiddling with the money-canister that zooms along an overhead pulley-system carrying payment up to Mr Bruce in the Office and down to Miss Beale in Lingerie & Haberdashery.

That will never do. I tug at mum's sleeve and whisper why we have to wait a bit. Then we stand outside pretending to be interested in the old cotton-reels and knitting patterns in the window till Mr Lee's got the pulley going again and hobbled back upstairs.

Then…

Through the door we go. I'm so excited I can hardly see or hear or move. 'Come on then,' says mum and up we go to the counter. Thank goodness we're the only customers or we'd have to pretend to be looking for a thimble or some-such. As it is, Mum's voice is modestly low when she tells Miss Beale the purpose of our errand. Me, I'm hovering red-faced, gazing at the floor. Miss Beale listens and nods not looking at all embarrassed, taking it all in her professional stride – 'Ah, yes. Now, if she could just come round the back to be measured …'

Measured? *Measured!?* This is not something I'd foreseen. My boobs shrivel by several cup sizes – which is good, but won't last – as I look frantically to my mum for rescue. Mum's eyes glimmer with motherly sympathy but her mouth's set in an 'Experts know best' expression.

There's an uncomfortable silence. Bra or no bra, there's no way Miss Beale is seeing my breasts, never mind putting round me that cold measuring-tape-snake that's coiled round her neck and over *her* board-flat chest. Loudly – and untruthfully – I blurt out: 'It's all right, I know what I am, I'm thirty-six … B' (I imagine C is as big as they come and no way am I going to admit to C)

I keep my eyes on the floor but I can feel the two women's pressed-together lips, the looks exchanged the solemn nods. Then a wooden box is slid carefully out along its grooves and tilted to be lifted out and set onto the glass of the counter.

Miss Beale's knobbly hands unroll each brassière in slow motion. Miss Beale thrusts her fists into their cups, spreading her fingers out like a starfish in a vain attempt to convey what the brassières would be like when filled by my breasts. The bras are all white and the only choice, appearance-wise, is lace-trimming or not. I don't want my mum getting the idea I'm after something decorative rather than useful so I point to the plainest one.

Would she care to try it on? Miss Beale enquires and I look down and shake my head while Mum asks if it could be changed in the event of its not fitting.

Miss Beale purses her lips long enough for us to get the message that I've been given every opportunity to see if it fitted before leaving the shop, then says grudgingly that it's not customary but she supposes so, provided it's returned within a week in the condition in which it was purchased.

Mum's turn for pursed lips. Oh, no! But – Phew! –After a pause and a sigh she swallows her pride, takes out her purse and the purchase is made. I can't believe it. I can't wait to get out of the shop before there's an earthquake and the building caves in or some such. But no, the brassière is modestly veiled in double white tissue and held out to my mum then, at the sideways tilt of her head, handed to me.

I have a bra.

It is in my hands.

Alleluia!

A few yards along the street we run into one of Mum's friends. There's no way I can stay. 'I'll see you back at home,' I say and I'm off on flying feet before my mum can say a word.

I race upstairs to my bedroom and take my bra from its bag. My fingers are shaking so much with excitement it seems forever that I'm fumbling and wrenching until at last, I manage to get the bra hooked at the back on the tightest fastening. A pause to get my breath back then I hoist the straps up and up as high as they'll go.

And then – for the first time in almost a year – I risk a glance in the mirror at that hated part of my anatomy.

It is covered.

It is snow-white.

It is form. It is not flesh.

I see a taut cotton second skin.

On top of this transfiguring, life-changing foundation, with tears of joy in my eyes I try on every blouse, jumper, frock and gymslip in my wardrobe and I find my reflection, be it full-frontal or sideways-on so very much improved that I offer up a fervent prayer of thanks to God. Oh. Is it blasphemous to be grateful to God for bras?

For several months my transformation is total.

Until one morning when I'm brushing my teeth vigorously and see in the mirror that the motion has set up a certain wobbling under my gymslip. I put down the toothbrush and touch. My fingertips have found twin crescents of blubber that's oozing out of the top of my bra. Ah, the straps must have loosened off. I hitch them up – tho' they don't go far and I force the bulgy bits back in. There! That's done the trick. But, a bit later, lifting up my arms to take my hair-slide out there's a sensation of upward shift. Now bits of me are squeezing out of the bottom of my bra! I don't want to look too closely so I do a bit of pushing, prodding and persuading.

For the rest of that day I'm really miserable. I hadn't even considered the possibility of expanding beyond the bounds of my miracle.

Over the next few years I save every penny I can get my hands on. Each new purchase promises to be 'The One'.

There's stitching in circles, semicircles, ovals; constructions with crossovers or cunningly-engineered sections bonded together for maximum separated cantilevered hoisting; there are fixed straps, adjustable straps, stretch straps, broad straps, narrow straps; two hooks, three hooks, four hooks; band of elastic below, no band of elastic below; productions by Kayser Bondor, Lovable, Exquisite Form, Gossard, Playtex. But nowhere is there the one that will give me fifties' tits: two perky pyramids on a level with my armpits and spaced some four inches apart.

Boys nudge and leer and whistle. 'It's just not fair. 'You've got it all wrong!' I want to scream. If only I

could have a placard – no; a sandwich-board, over my
front – kill two birds with one stone:

> IT'S NOT MY FAULT THEY'RE LIKE
> THIS
>
> WHAT CAN I DO?
>
> I'M NOT TRYING TO BE A COVER
> GIRL. I'M TRYING TO LOOK
> SMALLER
>
> THIS IS JUST HOW THEY GO

17

My mother said that I never should
Play with the gypsies in the wood.

Fifteen. And still I'm walking in time with that rhyme. I feel the breath-holding, the timing the run-in, the heavy turning of the long rope tensing the muscle of my right arm, I hear the swish of it on the asphalt, the chanting. Turning the great wide circles was the best bit. Not standing waiting to go in, everybody screeching 'Go o-on!' so you're afraid of missing the beat, that moment when the rope smacks the ground, frightened of it scorching your legs if you get it wrong, or being tripped onto your knees. Dreading the jeering laughter.

'Gyppos' Dad calls gypsies. There are gypsies in Rowell Wood but I've always known *they* weren't the ones we skipped about – the ones I knew my mum meant even if she didn't say the word 'gypsies'. Men. They were men; that's for sure, tho' the only Rowell Wood gypsies I ever saw were women selling lavender sprigs. The only suspect I can think of her naming is Sammy the Sweep – poor Sammy! – and there was 'Don't-take-sweets-from-Jimmy-the-shoe-mender'.
No mention of the Major. No mention of 'Uncle' Ecta. Too late now – 'mustn't speak ill of The Dead.'

Going past my old Infants' school I drag my finger across the padlock securing the heavy metal gates. It makes me shiver, takes me back to the bitter cold of all those iron-grey foot-dragging morning approaches ending in my small clutching hand being unmoored, my despairing gaze foundering on my mum's dutiful homeward back.

Ice-ages of bare-leg winters, chapped red-raw thighs, caterpillar-chilblained toes, alarming corpse-white fingers heating up to a scarlet banana-hand. Ice-shards in milk bottles, the baffling, enforced afternoon hour on an acrid camp-bed – wide-awake; why am I here? The rasp of slate-pencil on slate setting your teeth on edge, the clogging smell of old wax-crayon stumps and greyish plasticine lumps. I shudder – actually shudder – at the memory.

But ahead of me are the red doors of the fire station.

Ice to fire! How excited we were when that alarm blared out – it was the old war siren and the start of it would make you jump then it'd get bigger and bigger inside you pushing out your ribs till it climbed to its one-note wail you thought would go on forever.

Then, it was a bit like the Pied Piper – the running of firemen and children pouring out from all the streets of the town to be there in time for the clanging of the great red engine bursting out through those doors, always with little Mr Holmes – who lived furthest away –clinging on for dear life, still buttoning-up from shoe-hand to dragon-slayer.

In front of the fire-station doors there's a good flat bit where we used to play marbles – I only have to think of the 'chink' as one marble strikes another to picture my favourites – the ivory-white one circled by the scarlet moon-shapes, the clear glass one with a turquoise whorl at its centre, the jet-black studded with mica. I played marbles for hours – I've still got my most treasured ones somewhere in a small red drawstring bag.

The last house in the road, standing alone on the corner is 'Simla'. Mum told me that's a place in India where Major Fredericks – the man who lives there – was stationed when he was in the army. 'Fine figure of a man' they say of him because he's 'Major' and talks posh and has a droopy-down moustache. Well, I could tell them! My mum sent me round with a Victoria sponge when he'd hurt his leg a couple of years back and he said how nice and *plump* and *soft* it looked – which surprised me. I didn't know where to look and it happened that I fixed on the purple knotty hand trembling on his stick. Then he gave a horrible laugh and asked, very loud, 'Where's the wine, then, dear?' I'd got no idea what he was on about and I looked at him and was just going to say 'What wine?' when he lurched at me and I was backed against the wall. The penny dropped. Cake. Wine. Long yellow wolf-fangs bared. He-elp! No way was this Little Red Riding Hood hanging around in hopes of a passing woodcutter coming to her rescue. I was out of there – 'Major' or no 'Major'. I pushed past him and ran for it. Behind me I heard his stick hit the floor and skid, heard his cry and clatter but I didn't look back to see. Fine figure of a man! 'Gypsy in the Wood' Number 2, more-like. Mind it's another case of mustn't speak ill of the Dead – not that I would have; we didn't – 'cause Major Fredericks 'passed away' not long after the cake-fiasco. Nothing to do with me – a heart at-tack.

I don't need to pass the house today, I'm turning down Chapel Lane.

'*Da*-di-*da* di-*da* di-*da* di-*daa* ...' *Eine Kleine Nachtmusik* My favourite. The notes come floating out from the upstairs window of the Methodist school-room. The air is so still, the sound so beauti-ful. I find myself singing under my breath in tune, and time:

My mo-ther said
That I-I never should

Play with-the gyp
sies i-in the-e wood

In Chapel Yard a sudden strong shaft of sunlight beams down on me so that I feel the brown waves of my hair all turned to gold where it touches them. 'Flowing golden tresses,' I think. Like that beautiful singer from the other night I can't get out of my mind. I went – a bit doubtfully – to a Variety Concert with Mum and it was magic. You wouldn't expect anything like that in the Drill Hall – it's all fusty and the benches are splintery.

Jimmy Smith came on first, we knew his mum. He did tap-dancing, sang a song and told jokes about an Irishman, an Englishman and a Scotsman.

'Wuur, 'e airnt much cop,' they said in Howell. ''is mum were nubdy. Live down Gas Lane, they do.' (But a few years on he'd be Jim Dale of 'Carry On' fame, so they'd have to eat their words. Then they'd all be saying how well they knew him and how they'd always known he'd be famous one day.)

Well, he went off and the red curtains closed. When they swished open again there stood the most beautiful creature I'd ever seen. She was lit by a spotlight and had a pale-blue silky dress with a leaf-green sash. She made me think of a bluebell in the woods and when she sang it was like a nightingale in the woods.

Her name was Emily Chamberlain and she sang: '*My Sweet Little Alice-blue Gown*'. It brought tears to my eyes – the voice was so pure, heavenly. All the way home there was a voice in my head going 'Alice blue…Alice blue…' And I was thinking how I *knew* blue and thinking I could be Emily one day because it was my second name – when I was born. And then I remembered Aunt Zilla saying 'Mavis' meant song-thrush so maybe I could have singing-lessons and be a song-thrush. But then I supposed I'd have to stay as Mavis.

It's the way they *say* 'Mavis' here that gets me – half-an-hour on the 'Ma' and then putting in about three ys before the 'vis'. Take the morning after the concert: I'm lying in bed singing 'In My Sweet Little Alice-blue Gown' when I have to pull the sheet over my head and stuff my fingers in my ears so I don't hear my dad coming up the entry like Grendel.

It sets my teeth on edge, his Blakey-studded boots scraping on the stone and echoing, then the spatter of small stones dislodged by his broad black-smith's shoulders bumping the walls on either side. I think it's his not even knowing that I can't bear. What *I* love is to select a perfect pebble, slide my fingertip smooth over the cool and the curve, wiggle it like a loose tooth, prise it out and throw, listening for the tiny icy sound it makes when it hits.

Aagh! Another shower of pebbles. I'm should take bets on which'll bald first – his Harris Tweed or the entry walls. Hearing him lift the latch I know he'll let the gate slam, the latch rattle and bang. There he goes – slam, cough, stamp, rasp of iron soles on iron scraper and – wait for it …

'Maaaaaaayyyyvis!'

Is it any wonder I want to be Emily? I won't answer.

Another roar of my name followed by 'Oi, eyyu up yit?'

He just cannot cope with the idea of somebody who's not ill being awake and lying in bed. Bed's for sleeping. Not for sliding your legs slowly down against the softness and coolness of cotton that's been washed over and over, twining it between your toes. Bliss ....

'Oi-i…!'

Better answer. He just might come up.

His boots. Crunching past the bird-table, the dog-kennel, the outside lav, the coal-shed, the rainwater-butt, coming to a halt at the raking claws of the badger's foot nailed to the hut door. Inside the hut you have to duck under stiff-swinging or warm-dripping furred and feathered corpses with limp necks and open, death-filmed eyes, to get to the lovely smelling warm wood-blocks: the iron ball of the vice-handle hard in the palm of your hand as you tighten it. Steadying the saw-teeth on the wood; smoothly back and forwards. Sweet puffs of sawdust drifting down…

As if a curtain's been pulled across, the chapel yard goes instantly sunless so that I'm shivering, glad to be going inside. I push the door open and the piano stops suddenly, halfway through a phrase, yet I'm certain I didn't make any sound. No. It starts up again –

Beethoven's *Pathétique* sonata now. It's a mystery. How can someone so repulsive play like that? You just hum a bit of a tune and he can play it. Anything. With all the chords and everything. It's all I can only to pick out *Three Blind Mice.*

He's called Frederick. He's short and squat. His face is heavy and a shade of dull-red ornamented with a selection of spots, sores, styes, boils, warts or all of those at once. His nose is like a Williams' pear, teeth like tombstones and he's got so much Brylcreem on his hair it's like a field that's just been raked. That's just the way he looks. There're noises as well. He's always sniffing – horrible, big sniffs; and the way he laughs it's like a dog barking – or a machine-gun – and he laughs at things that are not a bit funny. But the worst thing – the worst thing – he can be playing something like, say today's Moonlight Sonata, and he'll be *chewing.* Toffees! Coconut caramels are his favourite. He's got a bag of them on the wooden bit at the end of the keys so he can reach along and get another without stopping playing. He makes disgusting smacking noises when he's chewing and because his mouth's open you can smell them as well, all warm and sickly-sweet.

Today he's sporting a gingery tweed jacket. With a tartan tie.

But just listen …

He gets to the end of the movement, his fingers come off like a bunch of bananas and he screws round on the stool. He says 'Ere, give us a hand a minute; this E-flat's sticking.' He opens the lid and I reach my finger over to hold down the hammer.

When I lean forward the curve of my left breast brushes against the ginger hairs of his jacket. It's like a doormat scraped over bare skin. I feel my nipple puckering and the skin shrivelling. Oh God, I'm going red. I'm so ashamed of my horrible sticking-out, getting-in-the-way breasts I'm feeling I should say sorry. Then. I see that Frederick's thick neck and ears have turned an alarming beetroot colour.

I'm standing transfixed by this transformation when suddenly Frederick gets me by the elbow and pulls me in close so my breast's firmly against him. Words stutter from him on a wave of sickening toffee-breath – 'I'd love to see them. Oh, *please*. Let me see them. Just *see… Ple-ease* … I'll give you half-a-crown. I'll … I …' His eyes are burning and sort of filmed-over. Mine are wide and dark with horror …

My mother said that …

I pull away. I stumble backwards, turn and make for the safety of the snooker room. I have to grapple to get the ring-handle out from its socket and the glass partition's juddering and banging. I wrench it open and let it crash behind me.

How dare he! How dare he!! *Him!!!*

And yet … and yet … at the same time there's a funny feeling; a stirring somewhere inside, in the middle of me. Sort of a bit excited. I can't believe it. I'm disgusted with myself. Angry. Bewildered. How can you possibly feel something that really, *really*, you don't feel at all?

I go to the back of the snooker-room. The piano starts up again – a Chopin Nocturne: *molto adagio.*

I'm safe. I walk around the snooker table like I always do on the way out. My hand dips down into the first pocket – the net's empty. From under the door to the kitchen wafts the thin, sour reek of un-rinsed dish-cloths. I focus on the wonderful clean white smell of the cottony yarn we knitted them from, the way it ran between my fingers, looping over the smooth, little-finger-thick wooden needles. I move on past the lop-sided hang of torn nets to the final corner. A great catch here – the brown, the yellow, the green, the blue, the salmon, the black, the white; two reds. I don't look, I touch; my fingertips sliding over the smooth, glossy curves until I trundle one, slide it down the insides of my fingers.

It's the salmon. The pinkness settles weighty in the hollow of my palm. Looking at it, by association, I find myself wondering … *Did he mean half-a-crown each? Or …?*

How *can* I have *had* such a thought? What is wrong with me? Yet, hamming it up in my head how I'll tell it, I'm laughing a bit. I'll say – *Well, I mean! You have to know how you stand in these matters. Half-a-crown each is a very different consideration from one measly half-crown. N'est-ce pas? Mais oui! And too, of course, what you have to bear in mind is that one side could weigh more …*

Bang!!

I jump. A gunshot! No; it's the outside door. Someone's coming in! I could stay but I don't feel like doing music stuff now. I drop the ball back into the net and go to the stairs; we used to vie with each other after Sunday School to see who could wing down the most steps – I was good; Jean was rubbish. You'd edge hand-by-hand down the polished wooden rails that squeaked from your sweaty palms, dreaming of breaking the 'seven' record … I'm going to try it now!

Suspended full-stretch with my eyes on the hollow of the final stone step the downward pull of my body makes me think of gravity and things falling … A brick. Falling… Nonsense! I swing to get away from that imagining and in the split second of my toes losing their grip on the step-edge, I see the white dome below. I freeze, remembering that other one at the Box Factory.

The surface of the Reverend F. Frederickson's head glistens with a cold-mutton-stew sheen of sweat, like it does in the pulpit when he's getting all het up about coveting thy neighbour's ass or whatever. Once I'd whispered to Jean – 'One thing, there's no risk of its dripping into his eyes and blinding him, it'll get soaked up by his eyebrows on the way,' and I said we'd bet sixpence on whether the next drop would trickle or get caught. Then we'd got the giggles and couldn't stop.

But that was another day. Right now I don't feel like laughing. Under the hedgy brows his oily eyes are squeezed tight together and sort of hot-looking. And – they are fixed on my tits. I'm beginning to pick up quickly on these things!

Even so, it's too late. There's no way I can stop my downward surge and the next moment – tits and all – I cannon into The Reverend, all but knocking him off his feet. *Geddin' ter be a big gel.*

'Oops-a-daisy!' he says, jokey, a bit breathless – 'Well! Well! It's a good thing I was here to break your fall, young lady.'

Fall! An 'eighter' that was going to be.

The force of the collision has pressed his narrow stoopy shoulders back flat to the wall. He's got his veiny fingers round my arm, pretending to steady me; they're trembly and he's got the thumb knuckle stuck out so's he can push it into my breast – the same one that caused all the trouble upstairs. He's shoving his pelvis against me then he smacks my bum. 'You're a naughty girl, aren't you – *pant, pant* – jumping down those stairs like that.' A corner of the Holy Bible in his pocket is digging painfully into my right nipple and even if I weren't too horrified to speak I can't, 'cause there's all musty blackout material suffocating my mouth and nose. I'm struggling, tears coming, trying to get my hands so's I can push against his Minister-black vest thing. It's then that I feel something hard pressing against the middle of my stomach. I'm desperate now, sobbing and I give such a frantic lunge that he'd be floored if he hadn't got the wall at his back. *Pity about that*, I'd think later.

I'm free. I look down at the doormat as if my life depended on it so that I can't see his loose-lipped mottly face.

'There! Alright now?' And shall we be seeing you at Communion tomorrow, Mavis?'

He speaks in such a normal, ministery voice that for a moment I'm tempted to look up at him in utter disbelief. But thanks to my loathing and my longing to escape from the disgust of him the Reverend F Frederickson gets away with not being looked at. Gets away with it all. As they do.

I fly from Chapel Yard, crying. The strength I had to use to break out of that vile pinioning has left my arms all weak with a bruised feeling down the insides, as if the combined weight of breasts, snooker balls and bald heads is cramping the nerves there.

> *My mother said that I never should /Play with the gypsies in the wood*
>
> *If I did then she would say/ Naughty girl to disobey.*

My fault, then? No. Hers – for failing to properly identify the gypsies.

18

Howell Fair

The following morning I awake to a fluttering expec-
tation in the air, a faint disturbance in the bed-frame,
the furniture, the walls and when I put my feet to the
floor I can feel a shifting beneath them, like I imagine
it would be in the breath-catching moments before an
earthquake.

Then, I know. It's coming. The Fair. Howell Fair
is coming!

Howell Fair is coming!

Nosing down the steep hill and on into the valley between our town and the next; vivid daubs of the Noah's Ark flashing in tantalising glimpses from between the forest-green wood- slats; it's always the first lorry to come and the last to leave, carrying the Last Ride of The Fair for when midnight booms out over the expectant town.

The Last Ride.

The Last Ride is free. Free and wild. Don't count the chimes and they'll ring out forever and you'll whirl on and on and never stop, the breath of the breath-taking boy clouding warm over your neck, his chest hard against your back, his arms and thighs pressing, enclosing. There you'll nestle small and protected as the hoofs of your painted steed plunge and pound through wave-trough and crest.

Faster … Faster … Until your gasps of alarm are no longer pretend. Down dip the lights. Speed overcomes sound. There is nothing but the rushing, reeling dark.

Faster … Faster …

On and on.

Forever.

On … On …

Never stopping. Never ever stopping.

Until … your heart lurches and clenches in panic as you feel the first snatch of the reining-in and 'No! No!' you cry, disbelief clawing at your entrails, springing tears from your eyes. No! Only seven short days ago that seem now seven seconds, those wheels rumbled-out the promise of endless possibility. And now. All gone. All over.

A year before it comes again.

A year!

A whole yawning year to wait.

Three hundred and sixty-five days.

No!!!

Slower … slower … slower … slower … and … Stopping.

Bright lights, jangling sound smash your sweet dark silent space.

Elvis throbs in confirmation:

> '… *down the end of Lo-onely Street*
> *In Hea-eartbreak Hotel*
> *You're gonna be lonely, baby* … '

And you do feel your heart will break.

19

Mother, Emmie

'Spose you could say I *fell* for him. Ha! … Double Ha!

I couldn't see proper for tears as I were getting off the Whip. She'd been gigglin' an' getting' up close as she could to him all through – me best friend! Mind, to be fair, you couldn't say he were exactly pushing her away – Bastard. Anyhow, me eyes were that blurry an' I were trying to get off quick so's I could get round next to 'em an' I were dizzy from the ride an' I'd had a few an' next thing I know I'm flat-out on the ground and them buggers are over there still laughing like bloody hyenas an' when they see what's 'appened they don't come over, just shout 'All right, Emmie?', so all I feel like doin' is to lay there an' bawl me eyes out. Then, when I try an' get up I think me heel's come off but it's me ankle – I'm twisted it or summat. Next thing I know there's somebody pickin' me up, putting his arms under me armpits from be'ind. I don't need to look round to see who it is – I seen this geezer watchin' me all the time I were on. Not bad-lookin', mind, bit like some film-star me mum used to have a thing for – Richard somebody – old, though; older than me mum I should reckon – mind, havin' me when she were six-teen, don't s'pose that makes her exactly ancient.

He didn't say much – shy or summat. Might as well get a drink off him, anyway; don't look like me mates are gonna be around. And his hanky that he'd tied round me ankle were good – it let me stand on it till the pain eased off.

Don't reckon he were used to going in pubs – a few blokes spoke to him – 'Ay up, George!' an' they all looked surprised –an' that were afore they seen *I* were with him – their bleedin' eyes were out on stalks then an' he turned me away, steered me over to a seat in the corner, hand on the elbow, all protective, like he woulda bin if he'd bin that bleedin' film-star of me mum's. I never said 'bleedin' while I were with him – he somehow made me feel I weren't the sort of scrubber who says 'bleedin' all the time. Well I'd got me first gin down an' he'd hardly took the froth off his pint – mind he soon got the hang of it – the third one went down in four!

We were laughin' and that when we come out an' I had to hold onto him a bit 'cause me ankle still weren't quite right. Then, on that last Noah's Ark ride – I dunno – with him so strong and warm be'ind me I couldn't stop meself sinkin' back into him; first it were like a little girl, feeling safe – not that I'd know about that, only what I read in stories! – then, somehow, it changed and I'm getting' hotter and looser all the time and feelin' his body harder and harder against me. I were just lost wi' the music thumping deep in me and the plunging up and down and the wild look of the wooden horse with its nostrils open, teeth bared with the bit between, its mane streaming and me plait streaming out the same. And his arms! Jesus Christ, those arms. He'd said he were a blacksmith and when I looked at them arms – huge, brown, hard – well, it were like I were swimming in a warm, dark-red sea.

He near had to carry me off – and it weren't 'cause of the ankle, tho' I made out a bit as if it were. I were gone. He could do anything. I just wanted to sink. To sink and drown in him. By now we were stumbling, in a fever, knees weak in our hurry to get there – somewhere as he knew – someplace called Fanny Joyce's Lane. When we got to the turn-off he stopped, said he'd got to ask me something. He said 'Are you …' and me eyes were all tears again 'cause I thought he took me for a pro and he was gonna ask how much but what he asked me was 'Are you a virgin?' and that made more tears – tears for being the sort as'd straightaway think he were gonna say that about being a pro and for how I'd got that way; for not being a virgin thanks to me mum getting the clap an' cryin' an' beggin' that we'd got no food money nor rent money and we'd be in the poor-house if I didn't let her regular Saturday nighter do it to me – just this week. Day before me sixteenth birthday it were – 'He don't mind the light off and he stands be'ind so you won't even 'ave to see his ugly mug …'

That's when I fetched her one – a black eye to go along with the clap she had then. We'd beg and starve on the streets, I said before I'd do that. But I did let me fella do it soon after – if that were what she thought of me, might as well. Long as I didn't get knocked-up – last thing we needed was another mouth to feed.

So, when he said that, I couldn't get a word out, just shook my head – you couldn't tell a man like him any of that stuff – Christ, he'd run a mile – if he could even believe it. Then he's lookin' into my face, all se-rious-like and I can't have him seeing bleedin' tears, so I toss my head away from him, pretending cheeky an' I say, 'Why? Are you?' An' I laugh. He ain't laugh-ing tho' – his lips are pressed tight together and turn-ing up at the corners and there's a sort of heavy breath comes out between 'em: 'Near enough,' he says. I open me mouth to say something but he puts his finger there to stop me. I know it's that he don't want the moment spoilt and I don't neither, so I get the finger in my mouth and roll my tongue round it and suck it. His face – my God, you should've seen his face; like he's bin struck by lightning. I could feel tears welling-up achy be'ind me cheeks. This great strong man, middle-aged, married years an' years, like this; with a finger! Christ, what would he do if…? Mind there's not gonna be time for that!

His cock! My God! It fills me and fills me so when he moves inside mc I'm back under the water of that deep warm sea, drowning and I hear my cries brilliant red. Then I'm rising to the surface. Light-headed. Smiling.

The man is crying; tears on his cheeks, arms dangling. Just looking into my eyes. Helpless. He reaches a hand to touch my hair, takes my hand and presses the fingertips to his mouth.

I don't have no cheek nor nothing for this.

The balloon he got me's flown up to the top of the tree, the colour of one o' them tropical flowers – scarlet, that's the word.

20

'Father: Unstated'

It were the last night of Howell Fair. I'm allus gone
down for the last night. Proclamation six o'clock of a
Monday morning; then the last night. That does me
now. Mind I used to be down every minute they were
open when I were a young 'un, an' every night when I
got big enough to shoot down the cans, knock over
the coconuts, roll up me sleeves an' mek the bell ring
wi' the hammer, an' the gels watching an' squealing
an'mekking 'em scream on the Whip an' that.

This gel were on the Whip that night. I'd bin see-ing her 'cause she had hair that were done in a great thick plait – honey-colour it were an' flying be'ind her an' swishing an' lashing side-to-side. The plait made me think o' summat. I thought a bit then I got what it were – that gel in the fairy-story as gets locked up in the witch's tower in the forest; its got no door an' she has to let down her golden hair for the old hag to climb up, then a prince sees this and she lets him climb up. Mind, I airn't no prince!

I never saw just what happened when the girl got out the car – reckon she must a' been all dizzy – may-hap all that hair swinging made it worse. Anyrate, next thing she were on the ground and them ones she were with when they seen she were pushing 'erself up on her hands an' knees, they just shouted summat about were she alright and 'See yer in the pub.' I were shocked be that – you wouldn't get none o' the gels round here expected to walk in the door of a pub on their own. And them going off like that. Londoners, I reckon they were. An' the one as'd shouted, he turned away an' were laughing an' took a hold of the other gel be the hand. It hurt me seein' the plait-gel's face when she looked over an' saw that; she were startin' ter crumple back down again, her head sunk an' the shoulders like shaking.

I went uvver an' put me 'ands under her armpits to help her up; she were light as a feather an' that hair smelt lovely – like honeysuckle – an' it were real soft when a bit brushed me cheek – there were so much of it an' it were so heavy I reckoned it'd weigh 'bout as much as the rest of her put together – an' the colour were in-between clover honey an' heather

133

honey. She were leaning back again me to get her breath back an' the top of her head were under me chin an' me heart were thudding away like the forge heating up – an' I were heating up too. Then she moved a bit away an' said, 'Thanks, Guv.' An' I said I s'pected she were from London. Then I couldn't think of nowt else so we just stood there. Then when she tried to move a bit, she shouted out an' got a hold of me arm – 'I think I'm twisted me ankle,' she said in a teary voice an' me heart give a great hot leap.

I got her to lean on me shoulder an' I took out me clean white hanky, unfolded it, folded it up diagonal like a bandage then squatted down an' told her to put the bad foot on me knee if she could, so's I could bind it up. I coulda' circled her ankle wi' me finger an' thumb it were that small an' that somehow caved in me chest an' I had to say summat but me voice come out all funny an' gruff-like when I said it were all the fault of the bloody silly shoes she were wearin'. I were mad at the shoes, not at her, but I were 'fraid she'd tek again me, the way it come out, but she nivver – she laughed an' wiggled the foot a bit so's the black patent flashed an' reflected the fair-lights an' said, 'Dontcha like them, then?'

Like 'em? Christ! It were all I could do to stop meself cramming shoe an' foot an' all into me mouth. 'Spec so,' I said, 'but they airn't very suitable for fairs an' that.'

Then she laughed again: 'Well, a girl has to look nice going to the fair – never know who you might find there.' And she looked down at me, all cheeky. I went red an' then I thought, she cairn't be no more than eighteen. And I seen meself – an old married man – a country bumpkin an' I told meself, dorn't be so bloody silly, an' I stood up a bit quick so's she had to grab onto me arm again. 'Is that better?' I asked her, an' me voice come out all rough. She said as 'ow it were a lot better but I'd have to help her down the steps. 'Are yer goin' to the pub to find your friends?' I asked an' her face went all crumpled an' she shook her head. So we stood a bit, then I said, 'If yer like we could get a drink in one o' the pubs,' an' I made sure it were in the opposite direction to where they'd gone – Reckon The Bluebell's orright.' She said that were a nice name an' that'd be nice.

She 'ad to hold me arm, walking, an' I reckon I saw our Zilla turnin' round from the roll-a-penny but we dorn't speak anyroad an' any'ow I didn't give a damn. There'd be talk, but then, when weren't there talk? Nowt else to do round ere. I 'adn't nivver bin in a pub 'ere since I were married – first, the Missus didn't like it, then I'm nivver had no money – and nivver really bin a drinking man. Rather spend me time out in the fresh air wi' me gun an' me dog.

When we got to The Bluebell I said I'd have a beer and' the bloke asked which one. Well 'ow would I know? 'Pint o' best bitter,' I said quick as I could so's she wouldn't think I were a fool. Lucky, they'd got extra hands in for the fair so the barman didn't know me – didn't want him saying 'Nivver seen you in 'ere before, George' in front of her. An' the good thing were, a couple o' blokes did give me a 'Wayup, George,' but they didn't say no more after they seen her – too busy goggling. I were that proud, puffed-up like a pouter pigeon.

I thought as 'ow she'd have a shandy or summat but she asked for a gin and tonic. Well, we had a few afore we left, I can tell you. She were laughing a lot an' snuggling up a bit an' I were feeling hot an' up in the air like. A red balloon floated by an' she reached to catch it but she weren't big enough. I got it for her. 'Lovely!' she said an' she wound the string round her wrist an' went up on tiptoe to give me a kiss on the cheek. I near stopped breathing I can tell you. I looked at me watch an' I said we better get a move on 'cause it were near time for the last ride. 'Last ride?' she said an' I told 'er it were a tradition – last ride on the Noah's Ark were at midnight on the last night of the fair an' it were free an' extra long an' everybody tried to be on it. What I didn't say were 'ow many years it were since I'd bin on it – not since I were married – near fifteen year. An' no kids to show for it neether.

It were wonderful. Wonderful. We were lucky to get one of the big horses – all flaring nostrils, and first I sat be'ind her, not 'ardly touching, then she said would I hold the reins an' I had to close in a bit. An' when it got faster she cried out an' leant right back into me an' I could swear me heart stopped. At the end, midnight were striking an' we whirled faster an' faster till I were reeling an' thought I'd die with joy an' all the lights went out when it were slowing down an' she turned round an' kissed me on the mouth an' I couldn't stop an' went on kissing an' kissing her when the lights were up again and I never cared if the whole town were watching. I knew this were once in a lifetime.

We staggered off, clutching onto each other an' I'd only the one thought burnin' me mind – Fanny Joyce's Lane. Kissing her all the way there. Hot night. And we did it. Me leaning again the field-gate wi' the soft small rounds of her young arse cupped against me rough blacksmith's palms. Oh, God! Grasses rustling, moon shining high in the black. Hot hot night. Inside her, her loosed hair spreading honey-suckle. Oh, God.

I know I should feel bad. Marrid man wi' a gel young enough to be me daughter, and a stranger at that. Five years I went courting wi' me wife an' we nivver got nowhere near doing it – and after, it was only put up with 'cause she wanted a baby; lyin' on her back on the bed, sheet down just enough, nightie up just enough, light off, mouth turned down, eyes shut, nivver a sound.

And this! Here. Like this. An' the moaning' and fast breath. The wild-bird cry. Oh, God.

Bad? No. I don't feel bad. Good is what I feel – good all through. I'm nivver felt anything like it afore an' nivver will again. It were marvellous. It were the best moment of me whole life. Glorious it were. Glorious.

21

1956

In the house on the hill, in a room lined with stale cooking smells, my dad sits at the table. His head is capped in his hands.

Below in the town it's the last, raucous night of the Fair. Gilded wooden horses plunge and rear; chairs on chains fling far out against the indigo sky; candy-pink crystals melt and spin to floss. Round and round. Round and round.

From this heart of light-pulsating music-throbbing darkness I have come here to this rectangle of dull yellow light.

Dizzy from love and roundabouts, I'm laughing. I've pulled the boy by the hand to wait in the shadow of the privet hedge while I tell my dad not to worry (and come looking for me!); I'll be staying till the end. For the Last Ride. My path here has been spun out from the web of the fair; a golden thread vibrating with enticement so that while my body's moving forwards my self quivers in suspension, poised for the returning.

There are sounds. Sounds of crying. Of a man crying. Slowly I move forwards and I see a hand groping the air for comfort, seeking me. The hand plucks at my golden thread, sending a tremor along it.

I just stare. Blank. Dumb.

Then. The words come. Choked-out.

Words that tear into me, spinning me plummeting to earth – 'Your mum's not going to get better, duck.'

No …! No …! Oh, no!

I'm not ready. I'm not ready. I'm too young. No! No! I want to stuff the words back into his wet squared mouth before their poison can corrode the channels of my hearing.

It's too late.

But if the words can't be rejected, the speaker can – he who made their horror reality by giving it voice. I back away, shaking my head, hands lifted in front of my face, palms-out, trying to push him and his words away, my mouth and eyes gaping black.

And then the thought for which I'll never be able to forgive myself sidles into my mind – *He might have waited to tell me till after; kept it to himself, not spoilt everything for me as well.* I shake my head to dislodge it, tears fly but I shall find that I'm never able to forget that the thought was there.

Such unnatural feeling at such a moment. The unimaginably worst moment of my life. Such callousness towards both Mother and Father. They've been right all along. I *am* no good. I am 'turning out like her.'

22

Fatal Inheritance

My poor mum. Sent home from hospital to die over a year and a bit. A time in which, the more her own flesh of fifty-odd years withers and wanes, the more the new-sprung parasite waxes to a smooth usurping sphere – the size of a baby's head. Where a baby's head had never nestled. The cruelty of that. One breast hangs shrivelled thin to the waist and the other is bloated so obscenely it's more terrible than you can imagine. I must paint it daily with Gentian Violet. *There, that's better.* A placebo.

On a day of lowering cloud I'd had an intimation of what was to be.

In the 'front-room: a glass-fronted oak cabinet where the Christmas-Day-only-bone-china tea-set is displayed – a wedding present to George and Annie (my mum and dad). On either side of the fireplace a brace of oil-paintings by Lilian Hetherington the local farmer's wife: one of a black Retriever, mouth stuffed full of limp partridge, the other a liver-and-white Springer spaniel with a cock pheasant's lifeless neck dangling like some gruesome discoloured tongue. There's a grate with a gleaming brass Companion Set that only gets used for brushing up the ashes of Christmas Day.

I'm sitting on the settee devouring a book, ready to stuff it under a cushion if I hear approaching Mum-footsteps. This book has been covered with brown paper and it's dusty from its hiding place behind the 'respectable' front of the set of Ethel M. Dell. The book is *The Blue Lagoon* and, being strictly taboo, is the book I most crave. But the settee is prickly and my painstaking search having failed to unearth any excitingly forbidden goings-on between hero and heroine I close the book in frustration. Upstairs under my pillow I've got the latest Dennis Wheatley.

'Mavis …!'

I'm halfway up the stairs, rooted to the spot. Oh, God! Mum's in the bathroom. Did I forget to put my away my 'thing'. Oh, no! How am I going to get out of this one?

My 'thing' is a pale pink plastic garment acquired in great secrecy through the putting-together of Co-op errands' earnings, the 'Christmas Box' of Aunts Zilla and Beat and withheld mites from the chapel offertory. The coupon for the 'thing' was furtively snipped from my dad's Titbits (Ha!) with scissors that I found – too late – had previously been used to de-rind half-a-pound of best back-bacon. The greasy slither of the blades and the fat white smell had brought the juices of nausea to my mouth but had also strengthened my resolve, being a timely reminder of that lardy layer of my 'too too solid flesh' the 'thing' was going to melt, thaw and resolve to a dew. This 'thing' – posted to my friend Jean's address – is, to the best of my knowledge – stuffed down in the dusty webby space behind the airing-cupboard hot-water-tank in tandem with an earlier purchase – the bathmat-like Playtex girdle whose claim is to mould any occurring excess of flesh into a buttock-less stomach-less off-white cylinder.

The rolling-up of this feat of American foundation-garment engineering onto the designated body area can be accomplished only with great difficulty, relentless perseverance and vast pothers of Johnson's Baby Powder. Should you be unfortunate enough to not get a good purchase on it at the first attempt *it* gets skewed and sticks, *you* sweat in panic and each frantic tweak earns you a smarting pinch from the spiteful rubber. More sweat, more tug; the bulk of the garment staying right where it is, the rim stretching and stretching, thinning and thinning over your fingertips like gum-about-to-be-bubble-blown over your tongue. Your fingers are sure to go through it in a minute but what can you do? You can't stay like that, neither in nor out.

But soon, soon, when the elasticated rubber 'thing' has done its work, there'll be no further need for these undignified contortions.

Oh, Happy Day! The pale pink cocoon will split asunder and the world will see that the fat white grub that dwelt within – bloated by compensatory bountiful daily-dolings of post-rickets post-war butter, beef-dripping, cheese, chips, ice-cream – has undergone a glorious metamorphosis ...

'Mavis!'

My 'Ye-es ...?' is strangled, barely audible; I'm picturing my guilty secret revealed in all its glory by the sullen light of the bathroom – the 'thing' draped over the edge of the bath like I've seen my dad's truss with its greyish-pink lump and, next to it, the boned, doll-colour contraption which in daytime hours contains my mum's amorphous breast mass into an unassailable rampart called 'bosom'.

'Mavis, come in here a minute, duck.'

Doesn't sound like her *trouble* voice. P'raps I did put it away after all. I take a deep breath and open the bathroom door.

My mum has lifted her left arm, pulling the edge of the interlock vest – worn *below* the brassière – into a vee-shape. 'Have a look at this for me,' she says, her tone determinedly matter-of-fact, her head twisted away from me.

I look. I don't exactly see anything but neither am I able to meet my mum's frightened gaze. 'What?' I say, almost querulous, idly rucking up the mat around the lavatory pedestal with my toe.

'Can't you see anything?' My mum's voice rises on a pitiful, self-deluding hope.

'No. What is there to see, Mum?'

'There's a … a sort of … well … a bit of a … hard ridge …?' my mum says then, losing breath, her voice ever lighter. 'Just feel it.'

Those three simple words. For the end of my world.

My whole being is a scream of 'No…oooooo!' A tornado sucks the breath from my body and the walls from their planes. My limbs contract in their urgent desire to flail against this maelstrom in a rage of youth and life. *No…! No…! Not me. No…! Ple-ease! I'm too young to know. You're killing my life. No…! I hate you … Go away… Leave me alone … Oh, Mum! Mum…! Mum…!*

I have to do it. My shaking fingertips skim the corrupted ridge beneath the

tender blue-veined skin of the breast. 'Mm…' The small sound I manage to produce is non-committal, almost bored. But in my mouth is the metallic taste of fear.

145

Mum's eyes search mine, frantic. What do you think, duck?'

The silence is the briefest of moments. Ages pass.

'It's just where my brassiere's been chafing … isn't it?

That small hardness has branded my fingers. Behind my back I'm scrubbing them desperately over the rough wool of my skirt as I say 'Yes, I should think so.' With a terrible, implacable, criminal nonchalance.

I am outside of the bathroom … I am outside of the bathroom …

Focussing hard.

That's it! The bathroom is empty. Of course. Scoured stain-free – bath, wash-hand-basin, lavatory. All gleaming. Curtain-roses blooming, towel as virgin snow, glass shade un-fly-blown, no primordial slime oozing from the sink-overflow.

The bathroom is pristine.
The bathroom is empty.
No-one is in the bathroom.
Nothing has happened.

23

Blame the Yanks in Winchester

But something *has* happened. Is happening. Day by day, all the time, that small roundness still presses hard against the pads of the fingers I touched with. And it's growing. Deep inside, secret and malignant, cells are multiplying out-of-control.

At last my mum goes to the doctor. Later she tells me and dad that the doctor says she has a growth. 'A growth!' I want to scream; anyone can see it's a *growth* – can see the growing. I realised I'd expected the doctor to have other diagnostic words – long Latin words – and too, Latin *cure*-words. My mum doesn't want that word either: something called 'a growth' *has* grown and *will* grow more. She takes to calling it a tumour; that gives people a way out – it seems they all happen to know someone who's had a tumour 'but it was benign', so not to worry. The word 'cancer' is known to us but never spoken – 'Is it …?' one will ask of another, who will press her lips together and nod gravely. The space of the word's absence is vast and black; it fills the cavity of my chest, squeezing my heart and lungs up against my ribs so I want to shout: 'Cancer! … Cancer! … Cancer! … Cancer! …' until all my breath's gone and I'm down on the ground.

A few days after the doctor, we're just going to start eating our liver-and-onions when my mum pushes her plate away; tears spurt out of her eyes and she shouts. 'It was those Americans in Winchester. That's what started it. It was those Americans.' And she rushes upstairs.

'Americans?' says my dad. 'Yanks? In Winchester?' He looks at me 'cause I'd gone to Winchester with Mum on that holiday to visit Aunt Edie. I look puzzled. I shake my head and say 'I don't know.' But I do.

I can see us, me and Mum, two tiny figures against the massive blocks of the cathedral, and the cathedral dwarfed by towering thunder-clouds, its spire a silver needle against the black. My mum's staring at the needle; she says it's a lightning-conductor but I'm just holding my breath, waiting for the cloud to burst when the needle pricks it. And the next moment it does and great drops of rain smack on the stone and sizzle and spread to the size of a florin bringing the wonderful smell of cold water-drops on hot dust. Then the rain's pelting down, hammering, and the bells clang out and into the clatter and splash come two men, as if they've been sluiced-out of some corner of the church.

My mum grabs my hand and we start to run for shelter. I'm amazed by the brilliance of the large pink flowers of my mother's dress blooming against the lead-grey of sky and stones. The men are grey too in their uniforms.

'Run it, lady!' yells one of them, grinning American-white-toothed, chewing gum.

My mum's bosom is on a level with my eyes and when she stumbles it jolts, then sways as she breaks into a gallop. I can hear her rough breathing and my sandals are barely touching the ground. When we get to the porch she's shaking and she bends over with her arms wrapped round her chest, so I'm frightened. What are heart attacks like? She sort of spits and I wonder if she's going to be sick, then she does it again. Then I understand – it's a word she's spitting – 'Yanks!'

I don't understand why she says it like that so I just look down at the ground and don't say anything.

Not long after we get back home my mum's really poorly. She's got phlebitis, the doctor says. *Flea-*

bite-us strikes me as a funny name for being ill but I'm too upset to dwell on it.

That was the first time she blamed the Americans in Winchester. For making her run too much and hurt her legs. That was how her first illness was brought about and this is her second, so the Americans must be to blame.

The thought does come to my mind that if there's any blaming to do, if my mum had let my dad see or touch her breasts it mightn't have come to this. But she didn't and he didn't and now I have to.

Have to change the dressings that mask the horrifying damage done by the Ultra-Violet rays prescribed only to pretend that something can be done to help her. Have to paint the blistered surface of the monstrous sphere with Gentian Violet. Which is a beautiful colour. Have to spend endless wretched hours on my side of their bedroom wall, listening for the dry cough and the painful creep from bed to bathroom, the splattering of my mother's vomit against the tin of the pail beside the bed when she feels too ill to get out. And all the time I'm burning with a slow hatred of my father for his callous, snoring sleep.

'I'm sorry, duck,' my mum murmurs in distress.

'It's all right, Mum; try and get some sleep now.'

Glad of the darkness hiding my eyes full of tears I want desperately to sound matter-of-fact, cheery; but that's hard to do with the lump in my throat.

The bucket emptied and rinsed, I'm left shaking. No way I'll sleep now.

At the foot of my bed is a half-moon Readicut rug strewn with the roses Mum and I pegged in curtained winter evenings. Those nights I kneel there, straining my eyes over the fine-print of the red-covered gold-lettered *Family Medical Dictionary* in a doomed search for confirmation that my mother's symptoms are those of tuberculosis – or of any other poly-syllabled 'osis' or 'itis' that stops short of the malignancy that dare not speak its name.

In Fifties Howell terminal illness – like sex – is another 'grey area' where the writ of 'calling a spade a spade' does not run.

'A growth' is the most I ever hear my dad say – the doctor's words of diagnosis he mumbles close to the end to an old friend concerned enough to persist. And the victim herself – my mum, who for forty-odd years has lived in constant and oft-voiced dread of inheriting the breast-cancer that killed her own mother – well, she has, by some quirk of her nature succeeded in excising all consciousness that such a disease even exists. The more hideously apparent becomes her condition, the less she knows. It's both pitiful and macabre – as if the tumour were in her brain, ever-expanding and nudging out the knowledge lodged there.

'It's a blessing,' friends say, and maybe it is but it places a dreadful burden of untruthful reassurance upon my dad and me – 'Oh, you're looking so much better today! Soon be back to your old self again … up and doing … out and about in no time.' And so on, and so on.

The dictionary definition of *euphemism* is 'A form of rhetoric by which an unpleasant or offensive thing is designated by a milder term.'

Howellians are past-masters of this rhetoric when it comes to their serious afflictions: 'And how are you today, John?' 'I'm bin better' … 'I'm a bit under the weather' … 'I'm a bit orff' … and – for the final phase of terminal illness – 'No. Cairn't say as I'm feeling so good today.'

So, having been exposed to such responses over a lifetime is it any surprise that when my mum's end comes I run from the room of rattling death crying, 'Come quickly, I think she's …' and stop. 'Dead,' is inadmissible; 'Gone' and 'Passed-on', euphemisms that have always made me shudder and vow to never use. And so my sentence is left hanging because the only other alternative that comes to mind is too preposterous to acknowledge, never mind speak. It is – 'Had it.' Oh, God; did I *say* it? I didn't say that. Did I?

To my own dying-day I shall wince with shame at this memory: not for the vulgarity of the expression but for actually being aware, at this, the most terrible moment of my life that I've been guilty of a verbal *faux pas.* Worse than this, I sense that while grief for my mother will dim with time I shall always have precise recall of how that jangling space behind my brow-bone echoed the void of my open mouth.

And, there was that 'No!' when my dad gave me news of the death-sentence on the Last Night of The Fair. Since when, through those long, long months of nursing I have cared deeply, I have suffered agonies but none of this can lessen my conviction of having failed my mother. At the end of her illness, as at the beginning.

I am no good.

My mum died.

QED.

Dark mourning-suits and ties for the men; women's smart black coats and hats, fusty-black vestments of the Reverend F. Frederickson. Him! Heads bowed beneath sombre cloud.

Cemetery crows, their wing-feathers fingers of funereal gloves as they sway on twigs no thicker than a quill; harsh cry and clumsy down, pinioned they wag and strut, make ridiculous macabre grave-ward, worm-ward jumps, carrion-beaked heads stabbing speculative.

When I step backwards the heel of my shoe sinks into the soft earth. I feel something hard against my stockinged heel, look down and see a white stone mimicking a skull in size and shape, a Black-eyed Susan twining from one of the eye-sockets. Gnarled rootlets of ivy are a hag's flesh-delving fingers.

Annie Lucilla Pilgrim
born 1899
died 1956
R.I.P.

24

The Devil and the Deep Blue Sea

It's me and Dad now.

'You'll turn out like *her.*' Him, roaring red-faced when I come home five minutes after the nine-o'clock curfew.

I know well who he means. And what – sort of. Usually this is where it stops but now Mum's gone and that means I've lost my ally, it also means I can take him on without her feelings to consider.

'What do you mean?'

'She was no good.'

'You don't know.'

His face twists: 'She didn't want you.'

'She did want me. She came for me,' I scream.

His voice which has become fainter by the word fades to whispering on his last two words. 'She came for the money. She was no good.' I can tell his heart's not in it – you could almost think he was going to start crying. I don't understand. His look begs me to stop. But I mustn't weaken – having got this far.

'Yes she was. She was!'

He changes tack – 'You're asking for it.'

'Came for the money?' Money? What money? And asking for what?

It. That's what. This must be the *It* that my mother – the *she* who was no good – was asking for. It seems that what I'm doing with my hoisted tits is *Turning out like her.* And *she* had a baby at my age. She was a bad girl, an unmarried mother, a fallen woman. *Getting into Trouble,* that's what *she* was doing. But I'm not doing *that.* We're all warned against doing *that* – mind, I've no very clear idea of what *that* is. But the being warned against *Turning Out Like Her,* that's just me and it's something to do with all the Howellians saying to my adopting Mum and Dad : 'You never know what you're getting' and me having to prove them wrong. Coming top of the class seemed to be enough at one time, but not any more.

It's all very puzzling. There are so many rules when you're a kid that everybody's always getting into trouble but I know this is something else – this GETTING INTO TROUBLE with capital letters – GIT.

I've figured out that doing IT could result in GIT but what is IT?

You know, Mavis!

No. I don't.

You do.

No. I …

Well. I know what they say *It* is and I've seen dogs. I felt sick. And there was his horrible laugh when Uncle Caleb said it was time to put the bull to the cow. But that's not *people*. I've seen little boys peeing up against tree trunks and it's a small white worm they're holding. Besides which, look at the Queen and the Duke of Edinburgh. They've got two children – fact. And they wouldn't do *that* – fact. So.

During the next few years I kiss as many boys as I can, but still I don't know. Until, one golden summer evening on the rickety footbridge at the bottom of the Rec when I get an inkling. I'm trying to follow the advice of 'Judy' in *Woman's Own* by gazing *up* under my thickly mascaraed lashes and deep into his eyes at the same time. I'm trying my best to do this when I feel something hard in the region of my tummy. 'Have you got a stick in your pocket?' I ask. Country people often have sticks for switching stinging nettles, or frightening off dogs – or bulls.

The boy with the 'stick' goes red and mumbles something. My words are hanging there in the air like the banner flown over the football-field on VE day. I squint at them. I know they're horribly wrong but don't know why. Though I am aware it's something to with GIT.

'Never do anything with a boy that means you couldn't look them in the eye if you met them in the daylight' had been Mum's watchword. But I'd *been* looking into his eyes – in broad daylight! – and it wasn't what I'd *done*, but what I'd said. So that didn't seem to fit.

Which brings me to my bra.

Now my mum has died it's guilt on guilt – Guilt that I agreed the fatal lump was her bra rubbing when everything inside me was crying, screaming. I went along with her because I couldn't bear to hurt her but I killed her. Guilt that I feel terror at being next in line to be struck down by the unmentionable malignancy – it has claimed my mother, her mother, her mother's mother; it must claim me too. QED. *But she wasn't your biological mother.* I know this, of course, but it counts for nothing set against my morbid conviction that the very abundance of my flesh is in itself an invitation to Fate: such an expanse in which to breed, such globular hiding-places – with so many existing nodules how could you ever tell the impostor, the rotten apple, the cuckoo egg? And it's a question of my just deserts. From my first mother, inherited depravity; from the other, untimely death. I flounder in guilt betwixt the devil and the deep blue sea. And my bra is my scourge.

157

Apart from the blissful brief moment when the morning-straps brush cool against my tender skin the torment begins with wincing and indrawn breath as they settle into their groove. From then on red-hot-poker searing is the order of the day with sedentary intervals of blessed relief when the straps can be slipped down – though, as with tight shoes, the price of reprieve is the agony of getting them on again. How I look forward to getting home, to the gasps and tears of relief as I ease my tormentors out of their angry crimson bed.

The pain of my shoulders being remorselessly bisected doesn't abate but I learn to live with it. Along with all other things, excepting my guilt, in the year preceding my departure for college the pain is mostly engulfed by the waves of my romantic yearnings.

I go to school, keep house, and dream morning noon and night of Romance. I accompany myself on the piano in songs of love; sing along fervently to *They Tried to Tell us We're Too Young/Too young to really be in love,* scan the pages of my *Book of Verse* reading of the tragic too-young Lord Ullin's daughter eloping from stern father to forbidden lover to drown with him in the billows of treacherous seas. I know that I too would gladly die for love. From Rapunzel through to Woman's Own. My current fantasy world comes through the letterbox every Wednesday morning just before I leave for school. Attuned to the very first rustle I start up, abandoning cornflakes, eyebrow-plucking, satchel-packing, whatever and rush to snatch-up the glossy rectangle from the dusty doormat – on one occasion I actually manage to retrieve it in mid-air.

There she is! Gleaming hair. Flawless skin. Wide *Gordon Moore's Cosmetic Toothpaste* smile. Wide, and wide-apart long-lashed blue eyes. Cover Girl. Role-model. Heroine. Avatar of love. Love concluded in short stories, Love ongoing in serials, Love counselled in articles, Love confessed to the Agony Aunt.

My passion is for the saga, going on and on with the promise of never-ending and the almost unbearable anticipation of next week's episode. Under the story's spell I devour every word penned on the subject of Romance and its *sine qua non* – Beauty. Here is where I shall learn everything, here the unveiling of secrets which, once learnt, will enable me to step into Love's story myself, as surely as any Fairy Godmother's bestowing wand.

YOUR FACE SHAPE

Carefully study the chart below.

Is your face round? Square? Oblong? Triangular? Diamond-shaped? Heart-shaped? Oval? Pear-shaped …?

Very difficult, this. No good ticking all the boxes – you'd never proceed from category to remedy. I can't decide. I ask a few people. Contradictory opinions. Seemingly my face-shape is too bizarre to come under any heading.

TIPS

Use a darker shade of Panstick down the sides of a broad nose to make it narrower. Under cheekbones for interesting hollows.

> *Suck in your cheeks, hold for a count of ten. Release. Do this in any spare moments.*

> *To keep at bay that incipient double-chin, slap smartly upwards with backs of alternate hands. Do this in any spare moments*

For increased and accelerated effect I do both together and sometimes stomach-clenching and ankle-circling as well – not those two at the same time.

> *YOUR SKIN*
>
> *Remember! Spotless skin is SPOT-LESS*
>
> *Whiten with lemon juice.*
>
> *Tighten with egg-whites*
>
> *Frighten (Ha!) with mud-pack.*
>
> *Soften with face-cream – Pat. Don't rub.*

Vanishing cream we use. On better days I view this as a magic blemish-banishing potion and on worse ones pray for a terminal vanishing. (Years later I happened to read the label – '*Absorbs excess oil*' it says.) Would you credit it? All those years of diligent patting and wondering why instead of softening it made my skin all taut and dry! I just used to put more on.)

YOUR EYES.

Remember! The eyes are the windows of the soul.

Bathe with salt-water.

Cover with cucumber-circles

Pat underneath with egg-white

Accentuate with whitening, shadowing, black-lining, red-dotting, six layers alternating talc and mascara - Dusty Springfield does!

YOUR LIPS

Remember! Lips are for kissing.

Using a lip-brush draw the outline of the mouth you want (So easy!)

Draw the outline in a darker shade, fill in with a lighter.

To make your lower lip fuller and more sultry, a lighter shade again.

Apply, blot, re-apply, blot, re-apply, blot, re-apply, blot.

Remember! Pink, not orange shades for yellow teeth.

Handy hint: Dig out unused bits in the bottom of the lipstick applicator with a hairgrip. They can be used for rouge!

YOUR HAIR:

Remember! Clean hair is healthy hair.

One hundred strokes at bedtime – to be taken with a pure bristle brush!

Wash in soft water.

Never use soap.

Rinse with vinegar, lemon-juice, beer.

Change your parting regularly.

Wash your brush and comb. No good applying a dirty brush to clean hair!

YOUR FIGURE:

Remember! Slim and trim for him!

Count your calories.

Cut out the starch.

Pummel and pound those thighs, walk on your buttocks, twist from the waist, cycle your legs, circle your ankles, balance a book on your head. (All at the one time??)

Wear a firm girdle. Put talc under it.

Stuff cottonwool in your bra for extra oomph! Put talc under it.

Yes. Yes. But how do I *shrink* my tits?

YOUR CLOTHES:

Remember! Clothes express who you are.

Wear matching accessories – blue and green, not fit to be seen.

Invest in a good costume – not black if you're under twenty-five.

Vertical stripes and dark colours flatter the fuller figure.

Be prepared! Never leave the house without a safety-pin.

BOYS:

Remember! You get what you deserve.

Be a good listener: watch his mouth closely as he speaks; it shows you're hanging on to his every word – and might give him the idea of kissing you!

(I don't seem to have the hang of this – they either get embarrassed or really annoyed and ask what I'm staring at.)

If he treads on your toes when dancing – which he will! – keep smiling.

Be understanding when he wants to play football or go down the local with his mates for a pint. Don't offer to go with him, stay at home and have supper ready so that you can be relaxed while he tells you of his evening.

Be reasonable – DO NOT arrange the wedding on Cup Final Day!

If you don't want to frighten him off don't ask him if he's serious.

Make it clear that you're not prepared to be a flash-in-the-pan.

Try to make him jealous.

Don't try to make him jealous.

Play hard to get.

Don't play hard to get.

Don't lead him on. If a boy gets worked up he may get carried away and be unable to stop. Remember! It's up to you.

If a boy says 'prove you love me' and 'Of course I'll still respect you', BEWARE! He won't. No-one wants soiled goods. After all, if you let him, you might let any-one!

Armed with such knowledge drawn from the fount of all wisdom, how can I go wrong?

BUT HOW DO I SHRINK MY TITS?!

25

Two Weddings

My mum had won a place at the grammar school but there was no money for her to take it up so her great-est wish had been for me to become a teacher. She must have been pleased that my favourite game was always *School* – with me as teacher – naturally! Well, I'd always known I didn't want to work in one of the town's shoe factories or in a shop or in an office – though I was made to do a shorthand-typing course, just in case. That was all I'd heard of, apart from nursing and I knew that even if I could get used to the blood and stuff I couldn't cope with washing people's naked bodies. So, it seems I'm to be a teacher. I find it quite impossible to imagine myself in such an awesome position.

My Teacher Training College is in a great park, high on a hill. Although the postcode is London it's a good ten miles south of the capital my dad deems the sink of all iniquity (where *she* came from).

I'm there only a matter of weeks – frightened of everything and everyone – when I get a letter from my dad saying he's married again.

I can't believe it.

I don't believe it.

It can't be true.

I'd known something was up when I saw the blue Basildon Bond envelope with Dad's jerky spider handwriting – he left school at thirteen and never writes anything if he can help it. Mum, and then me, had always done any forms and stuff.

He's got married again? And didn't tell me?

The breath whooshes out of my body; I have to sit down and my fingers go limp so the letter falls to the floor. But who would marry him? And where did he find her? Churning and shaky inside I bend and pick up the single lined sheet and read on.

It says she's called Doris. A widow. Originally from Howell. Left as a young girl, married a Scottish soldier and lived in Edinburgh with the odd visit home to see her sister Connie: 'You know, Mrs Coe up Harrington Road by Castle Alley.' I don't know.

Anyhow, seemingly on her latest visit – after *a whole week* looking after himself, his daughter having abandoned him – they met in the Co-op butcher's, got talking and went to the Chapel Harvest Supper. Full-stop. Love Dad.

I start to cry. Great racking sobs. I feel so hurt he didn't tell me. And ashamed. I'm not worth being told. Not trustworthy enough. His own daughter. Me and him going through Mum's death together and the year after, looking after him, and then it's 'Oh, by the way, I got married the other day.'

I can't tell anyone here. Who would understand coming from such a home! I'll have to pretend he's told me he's met someone who'll look after him but that he's been worrying about how I'll take it – that I've written straight back saying not to be silly and of course I don't mind at all, that I'm happy for him. (Like it should have been. Like I would have been.) Then, after I get back from the next holiday I can say about going to the Register Office – 'The silly old thing would wait till I was home for Christmas – you know how soppy and sentimental Dads can be!'

Somebody who'll look after him … Well, guess that lets me off the hook.

It's a while before I'm able to write back.

Alone in the world, rejected, an orphan once more, I am desperate to find a boyfriend, to get engaged, to get married. To belong to someone.

And so I – no; *she* – I cannot think it was 'I' –

And so she does. Oh, yes! Engaged in the final year of college, and – *reader, she marries him* the next.

She had found him. Her Mr Right. The first one whose hands didn't wander where they shouldn't. Who had Alice-blue eyes. Who believed in giving oneself for the first time between the sheets of the bridal bed. Who loved the passionate outpourings of Opera. Who'd sailed the Seven Seas – and painted watercolours of them. Who had been out with the prettiest, cleverest Head Girl they'd all had a crush on. Who'd chosen *her*, Mavis Pilgrim.

He whose facial rotundities were overlooked in the dazzle of the glinting fire of the band that was to encircle her left hand's third finger and proclaim to all the world that she belonged to someone. She, Mavis, has been *chosen*. For a second time.

First day of the honeymoon. The newly-weds awake to celebratory cloudless skies and hot sunshine. First breakfast together then it's off, hand-in-hand to the golden sands. Both are happy to be out in the fresh air, the ozone dispelling the cobwebs of the night before's shrouded unsatisfactory attempt at losing their virginity. No matter. After three years of saving themselves for the sanctity of wedlock there'll be plenty of time for that sort of thing.

Mavis will be glad when they reach the sea; her bathing-costume's riding cuttingly up between her legs and pulling crampingly down against the nerves of the back of her neck. The straps are tied far too tightly of course, but at least the major part of her excrescence is tucked away out-of-sight and the blackness and firm-stretch of the material is pleasingly minimising.

On the beach she undresses with all due modesty, careful to fold her clothes into a neat pile – he likes neatness – placing bra and knickers decently at the bottom of the bundle, wristwatch inside a pocket and anchoring all with her sandals. Mavis is determined this idyllic honeymoon memory shan't be marred by a scene. New husband's Alice-blue eyes scan the pile sharply but, unable to find any fault he allows himself to be taken by the hand and the young couple run across the gently-shelving sands to the sparkling waters of Barmouth Bay.

He wallows in. She teeters at the water's edge, her gasps only half-mock at the icy bite of the wavelets round her ankles. He wades on. Doesn't look back. So she follows till only her shoulders and bosom are still to be immersed. All is as it should be in the best of all possible worlds; the boy laughing, teasing, splashing, the girl squealing in delight and a show of protestation. Exuberantly she smacks the water hard with both hands, catching him off-guard, provoking him to cry out, dive at her, push her off-balance.

All of which he does. But he's unsmiling and she fears she detects a familiar note of anger in his 'Come on!' – a disturbing downward inflection between the 'o' and the 'n' as he swims off. A cloud crosses in front of the sun.

'A cloud crossed in front of the sun,' she says in her head.

Blinking back the customary tears, chiding herself for being ridiculous and over-sensitive she strikes out towards the sun which now glints once more on the crests of the incoming waves. Glorying in the cool and flow of the water against her strong but weightless limbs she turns onto her back, floating, becoming only molten sun and seagull cry.

Lapped by the ripples of her husband's return she plays possum, aware of him diving down, waiting for his hands to touch her wickedly from beneath, molten sun in her loins. He swims under her, bobs up on the other side. 'I'm getting out; bit cold,' he says. She flips over onto her front, anxious to swim back with him.

Her white breasts float out before her on the water.

There's a moment when she regards them as phenomena quite apart from herself before she realises what has happened. Clutching the top of her bathing-costume against her she calls 'Hang on!' while 'Let go!' tempts a small voice inside her. So she does. He turns, snapping 'What?' And then he sees them. *An expression of the utmost disgust contorted his features* she says in her head and to drive out this unhelpful perception splashes about furiously, grabbing for the costume-top, pretending it was all an accident.

'The strap's come off,' she says with a carefully small laugh, small shrug, widened eyes.

'How the bloody Hell did you manage that! Christ! Trust you! Go on then, bloody find it.' He stands in fury for a moment, hands clenched then with another explosion of 'Christ!' he's off, ploughing along, face in the water.

She's shivering. And crying.

Shiver and cry – that's all I was able to do at that moment. But later I worked it out. My sailor husband's last voyage had been through the pink-skied crystal South China Sea, jewelled fish at the porthole of his tiny, immaculately-ordered cabin, pencil-point poised over soft white pad to capture their quicksilver dive and dart. Contrast that day of murky confusion spawning grotesque pale balloonings, voraciously demanding what he can never give.

If only the song 'Sailor' *hadn't been No. 1 that year. If only I hadn't sung along so yearningly that I came to believe it: 'Sailor, leave the sea …' If only. I could have stayed his Madame Butterfly, sighing for those blue wafer-thin sheets addressing 'a rose born to blush unseen and waste its fragrance on the desert air' and he could have stayed all ship-shape and Bristol fashion. If only.*

By the time she gets to him he's buttoning up his trousers, his back to her. Turning, he avoids her pleading eyes, glances in the direction of the still-missing strap, lip curled nastily, saying nothing. Finished dressing he rolls up his trunks neatly in his towel and leaves her there. She calls his name, sobbing; screams his name. He doesn't look back.

Suddenly exhausted she pulls the towel around her and sits huddled on the break-water. He's gone. He has actually cleared off and left her there. It's the first day of their honeymoon. A bitter sound between a laugh and a sob comes from her mouth. And there she'd been thinking it was shaping-up to be a good story:

I remember the time your Mum lost the strap off her bathing-costume …

Ooh, don't be telling that …

First day of our honeymoon it was …

Jack!

Oh, Mum, you didn't! Honestly!

With the two of them in secret-smiling at what the outcome had been.

She stays on far into the afternoon. At first out of sheer misery, then because she doesn't know where to go. Literally. The shock of what's happened has driven the name of the boarding house clean out of her mind. She thinks she remembers the general direction they'd come from; she'll walk that way.

He's leaning against the wall of Idris View Guest House – arms folded. Neither of them speaks.

From that day on she'd often get location amnesia when she was stressed. Even in Howell after one of his 'dos' she could find herself standing stock-still, panic at her throat, no idea in the world which way to move.

26

Wedded Bliss

So much for the first day of the honeymoon. And all
thanks to her tits. Who said she'd got them all out of
proportion!

There was a reconciliation – of sorts; he, uneasy,
jocular, making light of it, she, lip-biting, nodding,
blinking back tears – her crying was like a red-rag to a
bull.

They applied themselves diligently to the landlady's evening meal of lamb chops, boiled potatoes, soggy greens under Bisto gravy. They took the evening air and watched the sun sink below the horizon, as seaside-boarders – and honeymooners – do. And so to bed with a closed-dry-lipped goodnight kiss, his sleep sound, hers fitful and nightmare-ridden.

Next day, as per his agenda, they climbed Cader Idris where she learnt that holding hands upsets the rhythm of one's stride tho' she has no recall of this having been the case on pre-marriage hill-walking excursions. And, of course, daytime ascents are hardly conducive to night-time mountings. Well, there would be plenty of time for that.

As it turned out, that night's mothy lip-contact was to be the last time their mouths would make contact. Ever. Never mind – God forbid! – his eyes or hands resting on any other of her erogenous zones. Yet *intercourse* would take place on a more-or-less fortnightly basis, prefaced by his query as to whether she was going to put in her thingy and consummated by her wifely-dutiful lowering of his Y-fronts under the bed-covers just enough for him to manoeuvre himself into missionary position where, faceless in the dark he'd move backwards and forwards a bit until, just as she was wondering if penetration had been effected he'd come to a halt and roll off. Mind, in those early days he was considerate enough to ask 'Did you get there?'

Get there? Well, she knew 'there' was the euphemism for 'to a climax' but she had only the vaguest inkling of what that signified. Her magazines stopped at stressing the supremacy of the man's needs, the pride of a husband, so 'Yes, thank you,' she would murmur politely.

Sex isn't everything, they say.

Her sole preoccupation during the first year of their marriage was how not to incur – or, having unwittingly incurred – how to appease, her husband's wrath. Terrified of the baleful glare, the roarings, the pushings and pinchings, the threatening fist, she'd never know she'd done anything wrong until it was too late. Which made disaster-avoidance problematic.

On the wider scale she was puzzled. She had been chosen – but for what? Why would you choose someone whose every aspect of behaviour drove you to a frenzy of rage? Of course, it wasn't that simple, but the see-saw effect held good – the lower down the one, the higher the other – and he had no way of being in the ascendancy through sexual power. But he had it easy. It hadn't needed a degree in psychology to swiftly get the measure of Mavis's self-esteem. Child's play: 'Get back to the gutter where you belong,' he'd sneered and the flinching and tears had told him he was home and dry – and had fuelled his fury.

But, Pollyanna-like she persevered: 'Our First Anniversary.' She smiled to herself, repeating it like a mantra. If she said it often enough all might yet be well. Mavis was certainly doing all *she* could to make it a success: choosing her words and the tone they were spoken in with care, scrubbing and polishing until her knees were bruised (a smear on the parquet having more than once been the lit touch-paper for an explosion) the wood burnished until you could see to put on your make-up in its sheen. And, mindful of those magazine strictures, her make-up was already on in welcome – likewise her clean pinny – apparently it's stupid and just what you'd expect from a slut not to wear one.

So. On the dot of six that Friday evening, dinner was ready and – vitally important – at eating-temperature. The clock chimed the hour, homing car-tyres swished and Mavis allowed herself a smug smile.

He came in the *back* door. Damn! Missed the gleaming parquet. A home-coming peck on the cheek and 'What's for dinner?' and, satisfied with the reply he sat down to be waited on, Mavis dished up and sat down opposite … *Oh, God! The iron! I've left the iron on.* Careful not to arouse suspicion by jumping up she pretended she heard the cat miaowing to come in. She'd just switched off when the roar came. Her heart leapt and her fingers jerked onto the iron. She stuffed them into her mouth then into her apron pocket and backed fearfully towards the wall. The glass salt-cellar bounced off the door-frame, caught her smartly on the rim of her ear and fell to the floor smashing to the accompaniment of 'Sodding salt's sodding damp again.' Hanging her head she didn't see the push coming and fell, sliding the full length of the ice-polished hallway and cannoning into the front door. *So much for polishing!* On which thought an involuntary spasm of laughter bubbled up and burst from her.

Scrambling to her feet Mavis surprised a novel expression on her husband's face compounded of outrage, puzzlement and unease, and this provoked a further splutter. Oh, dear. Features back in familiar 'fury' mode, head lowered, fists clenched, he was advancing. But her laughter had released and empowered her; for the first time ever she was not afraid of him though she did take the wise precaution of sliding one hand up behind her to check that the Yale was off.

'What are you bloody laughing at?' he snarled. 'You'll be laughing on the other sodding side of your bloody ugly face in a minute.'

He was about a yard away by now. Mavis stared into his face, her eyes hard and round as boiled sweets with insolence, disdain tweaking up the corners of her mouth, curdling her voice: 'Go on then. Hit me. I don't care. Hit me. Go on … Kill me.'

Confusion weighed on his rising arm affording her time for a considered appraisal of his face. Then, in a tone of sudden enlightenment, she pronounced: 'You're mad.' The delivery of this verdict propelled the arm to the required momentum but with just enough catch in the mechanism to allow time for her to reach behind, depress the door-handle, pull it towards her and step nimbly backwards onto the front-step.

Raining out there. Of course. Good! For once Mrs bloody B. was not out cleaning the windows nor Mr bloody B. mowing the lawn or clipping the privet – tho' doubtless watching from behind their lace curtains. Feeling oddly euphoric Mavis strode out in a purposeful way in the direction of Fanny Joyce's Lane, passing the seat where she'd sat with Sammy the Sweep on her 'Blue' day – a million years ago?

Soon she was limping; her knees were bleeding from shards of salt-cellar glass she hadn't noticed she'd picked up; her ear was throbbing from the salt-cellar smack, the backs of her fingers smarting from the iron-burn. The land was dripping and mournful, she soon wet cold and shivering. For some twenty minutes she went aimlessly forwards then turned back homewards. Where else to go? Nowhere. If she went home her father would come round and shoot him. And there was pride. And there was shame.

She opened the door gingerly but she had nothing to worry about, he was reading *Ice-climbing in the Highlands.* What a good idea! She'd encourage this hobby, indulge him as a dutiful wife should. She sat at the kitchen-table to make a list then went up to pack for their Anniversary trip to the Lake District.

The rain went with them to Ambleside and by the Wednesday it had settled into a continuous downpour. After a morning foray to Shepherd's Crag their clothes had to be wrung out down to the underwear. Even Mr-Take-More-Than-A-Bit-Of-Bad-Weather-To-Keep-Me-Off-The-Hills had to admit defeat.

Dry and warm again they sat for a while on the bed reading climbing manuals. Finishing his article on belaying techniques he picked up his Ice-Climbing book and said he thought he'd go down to the lounge where the light was better. Still three hours to dinner. The circumstances seemed propitious – didn't they? … *Why, oh why, did she do it?*

But she did. She said – in a most winning way – 'Maybe we could think of something else ...' And stopped. She was suddenly embarrassed, worried that he wouldn't pick up on her meaning, that he'd ask 'What?' But no. Wrong. As usual.

He was up off the bed with such force that she almost toppled off it. He was standing over her. Looking down. His lips came apart in slow curling disgust and the growled words churned up from the deepest recesses of his being – 'God, you make me sick. Who do you think you are? (Screech) Bloody Elizabeth Taylor? Eh? Christ! All you think about's your bloody crotch.'

The door slam reverberated behind him.

The following Saturday on the back of the bike it came to Mavis that when her female form was shrouded in her Barbour gear or swathed in moleskin breeches, 100 ft climbing-ropes and karabiners, all was well and they got along perfectly amicably. She'd put the principle to the test in the marital bed.

Out went the frilly shortie, the long black lacy nightie, (de rigueur in *Woman's Own)* in came M&S men's striped pyjamas. Size: large. When the forth-coming intercourse night was signalled she carefully did up each white pyjama-jacket button, including the collar. These remained buttoned throughout the activity. And so to the concluding part of the test – the other extreme.

The weather, this time, was on her side. It was on an exceedingly hot late August night that she lifted a corner of the snowy cotton sheet and climbed boldly in – with nothing on. Stark naked! It wasn't long before he came up to bed. As he got in a bony knee nudged bare flesh. The leg shot back, his head jerked round and he espied – Shock! Horror! – bare shoulders peeking brazen above the sheet.

'Where are your pyjamas?' Hissed.

Well, at least he'd noticed. 'It's too hot. I don't want them on.' She spoke defiantly.

(Threatening snarl through clenched teeth) 'Get. Them. On.'

Mavis got them on. The tests were concluded.

And so it went on – apart from those two weeks at the end of their second year when Mavis left him – with advance planning this time. And why did she go back? Well; firstly, he telephoned her at the school which was impressive as at that time telephones were not much used outside of business and it meant that not only had he gone to the trouble of finding the number but he'd exposed himself to others' knowing of this contact – tongues set wagging. Then he said that he'd been praying for her return – down on his knees. Praying! And, while this had considerable impact what really clinched it was his next statement – that he hadn't been eating. Not *eating*! (Such was Mavis' love of food that such a concept was quite beyond her.) Before she'd had time to recover from this bombshell he begged that she just come and talk and she agreed – it was what the Minister had been urging (not the Reverend FF but a new, young and handsome one). The Friday evening settled on he asked what time; she didn't know, whenever – Why? A pause. 'I just wondered about … if you'd be cook…' Mavis lowered the phone; it had crossed her mind that was what he was going to say but she'd dismissed the thought as unworthy – outrageous. And, of course, that should have been it. It would have saved four years, but *Che sera sera.* Instead of replacing the receiver on the cradle there and then Mavis spoke into it icily: 'I don't know what time. Whenever I'm ready.'

He was truly penitent – there would be no more rages. At least he's got humble-pie to eat, thought Mavis and smiled at her witticism. His expression betrayed that he'd noticed this but in the circumstances he knew to let it go. Mavis had one more condition: they would live together platonically, not man and wife.

They did not swing through the Sixties but motorcycled and mountaineered, amicably for the most part. Until a Friday evening towards the end of May. What is it about Friday evenings?

On this one it was warm enough for cold ham and salad which eliminated the meal-provider's concern that the proffered food be of the exact temperature for immediate consumption. And the Cos lettuce – Wow! A particularly resplendent specimen – would take first prize? Thick with crispy paint-box-green wavy-edged leaves, each meticulously cleaned … But no. No. Remember Sleeping Beauty and the one fatal hidden-away spindle they hadn't been able to find and destroy? So it was with the smallest of small white grubs that had contrived to secrete itself away from Mavis's attentions, manoeuvring itself tightly beneath a spectacularly tightly-curled leaf edge. And where did this leaf fragment end up? Where else? On his plate. Sod's Law. Every time.

A green-and-pink wetness slammed into her face and the plate travelled on to hit the wall and smash to smithereens. She sat unmoving, unspeaking, unfocussed as the gobbets of food dropped from her face to her lap.

'Get me another meal,' he screamed.

She did. She stood up, cleared away the mess, fried bacon-and-eggs. So much for salad days – literal or metaphorical.

The following morning he was up early, off to a motor-cycle scramble in Suffolk. He'd said he was sorry but she'd just have to be more careful, a man expects a decent meal when he comes in after work. (He did have the grace not to put *a hard day's* between 'after' and 'work'. (Perhaps he was inhibited by the Beatles' song.)

Mavis went downstairs, made a cup of coffee, washed the cup, fed the cat and left a note on the kitchen table saying that she would not be back that evening but would come the following morning. This table was hinged and she had strict instructions to always fold it down after breakfast but perchance when he read her missive her small act of disobedience would, for once, go unremarked – certainly it would, *fait accompli*, go unpunished.

Once again Mavis prevailed upon the kindness of her bridesmaid's mother in the next town but this time not for just two weeks. That night the familiar dream did not come –

The two of them are on the summit of a mountain composed of bricks, him looping the climbing-rope around his flexed arm, her seeing the brick next to the one he's on shift and crumble, knowing there are only moments before the next brick follows suit, knowing she must speak, continuing to watch in horrified fascination, only crying her warning at the moment his body arcs backwards into space and his arms fly upwards, his face a study of shock, disbelief, terror, pleading.

Then the awaking in drenching sweat, reliving the nightmare's images, recalling her Aunt Zilla and the brick imaginings that long-ago day.

Last night no dream. And for all the days to come no more dull throb of disappointment as she hears his car drive up each evening. Not that she'd wished him dead – on a mountain or otherwise – just for him not to come. Not to be there.

Her fear the following morning was that she'd cry and that he'd misinterpret this as regret at leaving rather than sorrow for the whole mess of it. But he knew.

'I want to go,' she said and he nodded, keeping his head down.

Post script:

Eight years. Of her life. Of his life.

Eight years in which he never even made a cup of tea – mind he did knock through a hatch, tho' whether to save her legs or to speed his tea?

Eight years and never a kiss or touch.

Eight years and never saw his cock.

Yet a couple of months later he wrote. Said she'd been the best wife a man could have, said not to care what they might say about her in the town, said he'd loved her dearly in his way. Wished her well. Said if ever she needed anything … She knew it to be sincere.

Then she cried. The familiar writing of envelopes that had winged over thousands of air miles, expressing such love and longing, that even now spoke of love after all the things said and done to the beloved. The total disparity. The impossibility of reconciling these states of mind. All inexplicable. And tragic. Yes, she cried then. For the mistake and sorrow of it all.

27

Intermezzo

Eight years wasted.

It's one way of looking at it but it wasn't my way. I was free to go wherever I might and if good things should happen they would happen in the place and at the time I'd arrived at so no point in regretting the events that brought me there. I was here on a river bank in full sunshine, moving through space on my own. Free as a bird – and the birds were singing. With me. The sky they were singing in was the very same blue I 'knew' that day in the Totty-grass meadow and the smallest, warmest of breezes puffed wisps and curls of cottony cloud across it and wrinkled the water. Water that was flowing my way.

Pink everywhere. Swathes of rosebay-willowherb patching the field, codlins-and-cream and Himalayan balsam edging the water-sheet. Stars everywhere – sparkles on the water, yellow-stonecrop spangled on my smooth warm picnic stone. I brushed down the crumbs of my egg-and-cress sandwich for the insects, basked in the high sun, flowed with the babbling eddies of water-sound. Bliss.

How to ever go? Force up your heavy lids, stir your leaden limbs? I didn't have to. But I always did eventually. The lure of walking-on would start to tug at me and it always won – or maybe it was a puritanical streak left over from my Methodist immersion – or the sudden cool from a cloud passing in front of the sun. Whatever; I'd broken the spell with my whys and wherefores so I may as well go. I'd do Ducks-and-Drakes first though – move, but not quite yet move on. True it's not so good when there's nobody to out-bounce but choosing the right stones is half the fun.

I very soon spotted the perfect skimming-stone: the right heft and of a size and curve to fit snug in my hand and along my curling throwing finger. I savoured the cool flat against my palm and then threw. Four skips. Doubtful I'd better either throw or stone. But I'd have one more go –aim for that dark reed-fringed rock islanded in midstream.

The pebble arced clear through the blue and struck home. Perfect throw. But … something wasn't right; there hadn't been a clean ring of stone on stone but a sort of dull hollow thud. Puzzled I strained my eyes towards the rock; then I saw clearly and my stomach gave a sickening lurch. My 'rock' was the drum-tight, belly-up carcass of a dead dog and my perfect stone had slid off into the seeping putrescence it had spawned. My eyes had grossly deceived me: they were nothing but bulging jellied lumps. Ugh! Hideous! I was choking on dead dog's hairs caught across the back of my throat. And there I was thinking I'd escaped the whole 'round-things' mess; standing there with that smooth pebble in my hand thinking how there was no ambiguity in a pebble.

And water! Clear. Pure. 80% of the planet. Life-essential aqua vitae wash-away-your-sins water. Water shaped that pebble.

Away with all rotundity, globosity, gibbosity! I would have no more of bald heads and breasts and dead dog's belly-bloat.

I would leave Howell.

Howell. Short for Hothwell: *At the spring in the heather.* Heather long gone. Spring long dried up.

Howell. Where the motto is *Wurr, goddalarf entcha? Cairngrumble canyer?* Sounds a very positive outlook on life doesn't it? But the fact is, these merry Midlands philosophers are forever *gooin' on, moanin', bein' mardy.* It's a sine qua non – you have to be disgruntled to live here – anybody showing signs of being gruntled would be eyed with great suspicion.

'Did you hear – Ole Frenchy took a potshot at her; shot half his foot off. Took him up orspital.' *Wuur, goddalarf entcha.*

'An' that gel as is been in the 'ardware thirty years could 'ave got married and gone New Zealand but she never got the letter an' seeing as 'ow they 'ad words afore he left he thought she didn't want nowt to do with him so after a bit he give up and shacked up wi' some girl out there.' *Wuur, goddalarf entcha.*

'An' ole Fred Cox, no sooner married at last than he ups an' has a stroke. He! He! Too much for him.' *Wuur, goddalarf entcha*

Howell. Pronounced 'Hole'

28

Metamorphoses

No more a square peg in Howell-pronounced-Hole. Mavis has wriggled free. She is off. Over the hills and far away. To a new life. In a new place. With a new name.

Attic-rummaging alone in the house after her Mum died she'd found her original Birth Certificate naming her *May Emily Stonebridge*. Her heart lurched, flooded her cheeks with crimson, took away her breath. *Emily.* She could be *Emily.* She'd thought of 'May' for Mavis for the time being but was resolved on Emily someday– like Emily Bronte; like that beautiful fragile creature who'd materialised in her class mid-term from living in Singapore. It'd been beyond Mavis's imagining that an English person might live in another country. Where was Singapore? And how beautifully this girl had spoken.

But when the new-name time came Mavis saw that she couldn't be 'Emily'. What a betrayal of her mum it would be to change back to the name bestowed by a mother who'd abandoned her. And, thinking so, Mavis saw a way to not only honour her mum but to right the wrong perpetrated by the Howellians who'd truncated to monosyllabic 'Nance' the lovely 'Annie', losing the open 'A' of its beginning, the lengthened 'e' of its close. Could two names sound more different?

Mavis ran a finger down the TES *TEFL Teachers Wanted* ads: the only one with any appeal being in a Bavarian town. She looked it up in her encyclopaedia: 'The last navigable port of the Danube.' The phrase appealed and without realising, Mavis was tra-la-ing the opening of the *Blue Danube Waltz.*

She would go. She would be newly-christened 'Annie' in Regensburg – ancient Ratisbon – the last navigable port of the Danube.

En-ferried and en-trained Annie went to teach English in the Rote Hahnen Gasse Sprachenschule, Regensburg, Bayern.

And so did Gabriel. A mere seven days later.

Never having heard his name outside of the Bible Annie called him 'Archangel', except on a flying-in-the-face-of-Fate Friday 13th ten months later when each exchanged most glad connubial 'Ich will's beneath the outspread wings of the German Eagle in a medieval Bavarian Rathaus.

So easy.

So right.

Headed for Gabriel's home town of Belfast, the newly-weds detoured to see Annie's Dad and step-mother, Doris in Hothwell where Gabriel was initiated into the arcane rural English delights of Cheeses in the Bluebell Inn – 'cheeses' being ninepins you tried to knock over by skimming flat round wooden 'cheeses' – and to a cricket-match on the village green.

After this Annie was taking Gabriel to visit her Aunt Zilla who now lived alone since the death of Aunt Beat. Though there had been a falling-off in Annie's visits dating from the 'Brick Murder' day and afterwards for all sorts of reasons, they'd always exchanged Christmas and Birthday cards and Annie had sent postcards from abroad – the last one bearing the good tidings of her wedding! This one brought an answering telegram: SO VERY PLEASED FOR YOU STOP THIS ONE WILL BE BETTER STOP

Annie, who'd never told anything, was moved to tears by her aunt's intuition of the woes of the first marriage and by her prediction for this one.

In Annie's waking dream her Aunt Zilla's face is framed in the casement window, the fingers of her ghastly-white hand curled below, hovering above the brick. In vain Annie struggled to wake fully as the whole scene was played out again before her eyes: a small cloud of pothery-red dust is shed from the brick in its rapidly accelerating motion to its bald-head target…

As always in a dream Annie was jolted awake before the moment of impact and lay still as a statue, scarcely drawing breath.

… Suppose I told her? Told her today. Told her what I saw. That I saw her at the window. That I saw the brick falling towards Uncle Hector's head. That I thought she pushed the brick … I *saw* you! I *saw* you! I saw you push a brick onto Uncle Hector's head and kill him …

At two o'clock that afternoon Annie rang the bell of the Milland Residential Home: red-brick Victorian, manicured lawn, flowerbeds gaudy with scarlet salvias and carmine begonias, assorted gnomes fishing in the one-goldfish pond.

The door- chimes' tinkle is '*Jerusalem*'. And did those feet in ancient time walk …? Annie gave a wry look at the abandoned Zimmer frame askew by the steps leading up to the front door.

Muffled sounds, a moving figure glimpsed through floral frosted glass – recognizably female. By the time she opened the door Annie had worked some more on what she imagined to be a 'visiting-relative' smile, feeling the result to be a ludicrously unconvincing ingratiating/apologetic combination.

Mildred. Jet-dyed hair piled above gold-rimmed rose-tinted spectacles, a flouncy-bowed Terylene blouse with deeper salmon gold-edged buttons, American-Tan-nylonned skittle legs ending in 3-inch-heeled peep-toed pillar-box red patent leather overflowed by puffed foot-flesh. Was it the pain of this footwear or Mildred's precarious perch that prompted her knuckle-whitening purchase on the door-jamb?

Mildred spoke à la Sybil Fawlty – just in case this should turn out to be a moneyed relative: '*Do* come in. *So* sorry to have kept you waiting on the doorstep. One of my ladies trying to escape again.' Her confiding chuckle was followed by a hasty addendum, lest the visitors infer a disgruntled inmate – 'Oh, only to the garden. Live out there, she would if she had her way.'

Little chance of that, thought Annie, and then saw the old woman, feet planted apart rooted between outer and inner door.

'Come along, Polly. In we go. Who's a naughty girl, then?'

Annie was glad to see that this false-voiced wheedling fell on deaf dears. The shrug the old lady gave to rid herself of Mildred's guiding hand would have done credit to an Amazon. Mildred's small laugh of complicity issued from between gritted teeth – an undignified tussle in which she might well not gain the upper hand would hardly impress.

Annie saw the old woman's skull, eggshell-pale and fragile beneath the sparse wisps of ashy hair, some straggling halfway down the ninety-year stoop of her back, the ends still coppery. The pathos of these incongruous strands twisted inside Annie.

'Won't let anyone cut it, you know. I mean, we have the hairdresser come every Tuesday – Joan, lovely girl. All my other ladies love it – but not her, not Polly. Oh no. Have to take the scissors to her when she's in the Land of Nod one night!' Mildred spoke in a stage-whisper, baring her teeth at this sally and Annie didn't doubt she just might do that.

Angry with herself that her staring had seemed to make her Mildred's accomplice Annie was fantasising telling her she'd cheerfully beat her to death with the woman's walking-stick before she should come within an inch of her when Mildred lurched towards Gabriel, pointing out the newly-installed light-plastic-'wood' handrails on the staircase. She pulled a face: 'Them old ones. So nasty and dark. And you've got to keep woodworm in mind.'

Annie saw Gabriel was struggling to suppress a laugh but he needn't have worried, Mildred had moved on to shrilly extolling the glories of the florid-stain-resisting stair-carpeting, the wipe-ability of the rampantly-flowering wall-paper, the Supergloss Brilliant White that had so *transformed* that dull old oak-panelling, the *washability* of the laminate that had replaced that nasty 'parky' – 'A devil to polish, that was.'

This last provoking a small groan from one-time furniture-restorer Gabriel, Annie judiciously turned from him to find Mrs Campion's gaze upon her. Annie smiled, said: 'The garden's lovely now.'

The old lady seemed not to have heard. Deaf, perhaps?

A pause, a smile, and then she said, 'Campanula ranuncula ... Rampion ... Rapunzel ... Bellflower.' And asked: 'Are the bellflowers out yet?'

Annie smiled, said she hadn't noticed but would look when she went outside. The old lady nodded and Annie saw who she was.

She raised a hand towards Annie's auburn-dyed hair – 'It's an echo of your eyes,' smiled her old teacher, Mrs Campion, she of *Rapunzel*-reading fame.

'Thank you' said Annie quietly and touched Mrs Campion's gnarled, translucent hand. It was exactly what she'd thought when the hairdresser had invited her to take a look in the mirror that first time. Annie felt her tears sting.

29

Revelation

Annie twisted the door-handle cautiously, pushed the door hesitantly. It had been a long time and she hadn't been able to quite shake-off the night before's unbidden and disturbing notion of provoking her aunt to revelation.

As she moved forwards the face turned towards her could have been that of any elderly woman but as she drew closer it morphed into the features of her beloved Aunt Zilla, the gladness in her smile, quite overlaying that haunting face-at-the-window image and scattering it to dream-wisps, on the words 'Hello, Aunt Zilla.'

Her aunt's response was characteristically oblique – 'I love the colour of your hair … more amber than auburn … topaz …?'

The same old affinity! 'Thank you, aunt! With your seal of approval I shall spurn and scorn any opposing opinion.'

Zilla laughed: 'Well, aren't I the important one!'

'A little bird told me you were deaf as a post.' Annie raised her eyebrows.

'Mmm … you can say "stone-deaf" but not "post-deaf"', Zilla observed. 'Pity.' I quite fancy "post-deaf". I might say "post-deaf" from now on.'

'But you're *not*,' pointed out Annie, laughing. 'Neither "stone" nor "post"'.

'None so deaf as those as won't hear.'

'As your mother used to say.'

'Good Lord! Fancy you remembering that. Mind, I don't think mother meant me to take it as *good* advice!' She leant forwards, placing a craggy hand on Annie's knee, lowering her voice confidentially: 'I tell you, Mav.. sorry …'

'No, don't be silly. Call me Mavis, like you always did.'

'I shall do no such thing. Annie you are now, so Annie I'll call you. It goes so much better with the hair – and it makes me think of your mum. Not to mention keeping my wits about me. More testing than a crossword I reckon – people changing names. As I was saying, most of what you hear in here would freeze the blood in your veins; turn your bones to stones if you let it get through. Mind, I have to admit I did get the occasional deaf-spell even while your aunt Beat was alive.'

Annie gave a shout of laughter. '*Really?* What a terrible shame!'

With a mischievous smile Zilla pulled a hearing-aid from her pocket. 'Look what I've fished out especially for you – in case anyone catches us talking nineteen to the dozen. A bit hard to explain if I haven't got it in.'

Laughing with her aunt Annie couldn't imagine how the idea of confronting her with 'the brick day' could have even come into her head, never mind …

'Where's this new husband of yours, then?' Zilla was asking. 'He's better than the other one, I'll be bound.'

Annie smiled: 'Oh yes! He's wonderful.' Again, the perfect note struck – acknowledgement of the first marriage's failings – of which she'd given no detail – without any undue sympathy or curiosity. 'But it's you I've come to hear about – how you cope in here – if it's bearable.'

Zilla reassured her. 'Switching-off' has been her salvation; plus she listens to endless Radio 4 above and under the bedclothes, plots lurid sticky-ends for Mildred and sits in the garden under the willow tree every moment they'll let her.

Annie asked if scyllas grew there and her aunt's eyes brimmed with sudden tears – 'You remember the scyllas …?'

In a parody of mouth-pursed, brow-knotted concentration Annie looked skywards as if to seek inspiration – 'Scyllas…? Scyllas…? Er… let me think … Aah … Flowers! Small. Blue. Flowers!'

Her aunt's smile told Annie she was grateful to be rescued from any wallowing in sentiment – never her style; she'd deem it a sign of failing powers to fall into it now.

'Annie,' said Aunt Zilla, and her tone was urgent, her eyes staring. Annie's heart missed a beat – was she about to be told of something dreadful, something that would change everything, some terminal illness? She struggled to keep her face from registering her dismay, to say 'Yes?' lightly.

Zilla drew in a deep breath, then 'You remember the Box Factory?' The words, tho' spoken so softly, slammed into Annie like a ten-ton truck. The eyes she raised to her aunt were dilated black, even as she told herself 'Don't be ridiculous, she just means do you remember the Box Factory?'

'You were there. That day. I saw you.'

Annie struggled for breath to speak. Then 'Yes … yes … Saturdays. I used to come every Saturday.' She forced a bright smile.

'The Saturday Hector –' pause, a glimmer of a smile '– dropped dead.'

Annie could only stare, heard herself whimper … 'Heart attack.'

'Heart?' echoed her aunt. 'Hector's heart – that's a good one. Let me tell you, Annie. I have to tell you. I need to tell you …'

Only with the most colossal effort of will does Annie manage to keep her hands from flying up to her ears to block out the terrible words she dreads are to come. She is staring at her aunt, mesmerised as a rabbit before a stoat. Rendered speechless.

Zilla goes on. Tonelessly but oh, so clearly: 'He only bothered to come because it was on his way home from the Conservative Club. Pints he'd poured and slobbered down him. Couldn't even be bothered to take hisself as far as the closet down the bottom of the yard…'

A hand goes up to cover the listener's mouth, tears spring to her eyes but her aunt is relentless. Cannot stop.

'Unbuttoning himself there. A steaming yellow stream. Like an old carthorse in the street' – her aunt crying now – 'splashing all over my gillivers as I call wallflowers from Shakespeare's word and that smell like prunes. And when I thought of Shakespeare I was thinking of Romeo and Juliet. And he was wiping his pissy fingers on his stinking trousers and rubbing the snot from his nose with the back of his hand, and I remembered the time I'd missed out a pillow-case from the washing bundle he brought every week and he'd said I'd feel the back of his hand. And what tipped me over the edge was I was looking down on his lardy white head ...'

She pauses. Annie is at first unable to speak.

Then: 'And you ... you ...?'

'Yes. I pushed the brick. My hand had been resting on it, the fingers tightening when he ...I remember I'd turned away in disgust ...'

Silence again. 'So you didn't see ...'

After some thought her aunt replies: 'I don't think it crossed my mind there was anything *to* see. Not much chance of a killer blow. Mind, the thing is, I know I'd have done it anyway. I wished I had aimed it. Yes...'

At which point the new husband knocks.

Annie went back with Gabriel to see Aunt Zilla before they flew to Ireland. She couldn't bear for that to be the last thing they'd spoken of.

Neither she nor Zilla mentioned 'the brick day', tho' Annie could tell her aunt was relieved to have unburdened herself – and she too was glad for the closure. She supposed she should feel shocked but now that it was told it made sense. And it was consigned now to the past, where it belonged.

Before leaving they walked around the garden. Over by the hawthorn hedge Annie found bellflowers: 'Campanula Rapuncula' – Rampion – Rapunzel in

German,' she told Gabriel. 'Rapunzel was my favourite story.'

Parting from Mildred Annie handed her a folded sheet of paper marked 'Mrs. Campion'. No way she'd be able to resist the urge to read it before handing it over! Annie savoured her thrill of pleasure at the thought of Mildred's aggrieved disappointment when she read the message inside – 'Rapunzel is in flower.'

30

Annie 1970

I am feeling very ill.

I am marooned.

On a hospital bed.

High. Stark. White.

A drip immobilises my left arm.

My right lies limp and pallid on the snowy sheet.

Taped to my nose is a transparent plastic tube.

The tube is threaded through my nasal passages.

It snakes down my throat.

Expanding… Expanding… Like a puff adder.

My throat is so sore.

My breasts are being milked. By a suction device.

The device sucks, squeezes, pains.

Will a baby's mouth feel like this?

I am feeling very ill.

I am helpless.

I am reduced to a function…

Not reduced.

Elevated.

My function is to provide

precious, life-giving milk for my tiny, tiny child.

I must be made well.

I am a mother.

I am feeling very ill.

I am feeling very happy.

Utterly, overwhelmingly happy.

Spread-eagled here.

'Reduced' to a function? No. Enhanced to a function.

One single function. Liberated from all else.

This feeling so ill is a dense blanket of fog, protecting me; it lets through only one chink of light from the world beyond – the insistent signal of my child's need. The only response required from me is to lie submissive.

To simply function.

My life is atrophied to a wondrous simplicity: mind in limbo, face (unprecedently) unadorned – unguarded, body whited-out.

And – *most glorious* to contemplate – for the very first time, there is no ambiguity in my breasts.

No remorseless euphemistic 'developing', 'geddin' a big gel', 'big up top' – no tits, knockers, Bristols, bosom, boobs; no 'nice pair' of anything. Neither wanton invitation. Nor craven shame. All bets off.

Simply: rounding out my hospital gown are the engorged glands with which a female mammal is endowed for the purpose of producing milk to succour her newborn offspring – their size of no consequence, their shape or perkiness immaterial. They function. That's all. End of.

I am so very happy.

Between my hips a new planet waxed and, cradled by a sustaining sea, my baby grew.

And the planet had two moons which also waxed, and their canals flowed with a bounteous elixir of life.

And when the time was ripe there came great upheavals at the heart of the new planet and my child was expelled protesting into the waiting hands of its new world. And the globe of the new planet was no more, but the echoes of its great curve could be discerned in the spheres and orbs of my daughter's perfection: fingertips, toe-tips, knee-rounds, buttocks, cheeks.

Heart-twisting roundnesses. And a pristine softness of skin you could never conceive. The conjunction of the curves of that thistledown head and my cradling palm is the sweetest, most poignant sensation in the world.

Smiling tears at the tiny defenceless head ludicrously dwarfed by a great milk moon I push back with a first finger the superfluity of flesh that threatens to engulf my baby, as if I'd done it a thousand times before.

When a nurse had asked who might give breast-feeding a go, I'd felt smugly superior to those oh-so-uninformed, so-young women with their curved, lightweight, non-wind, easy-clean bottles lined up beside the sterilising unit who were shaking their heads categorically, lips primly pursed as if they were being canvassed on the likelihood of their signing up for a cannibal orgy. Knowing mother's milk was making a comeback I got myself in the nurse's good books with a modest, if hesitant 'I'd like to give it a try.' True, I was shit-scared, but I did mean it, even tho' my squeamish unnatural flesh had begun to creep at the thought of loose wet leeching lips and pink gums. But somewhere in me was a hope I'd master my revulsion when it came to it.

And now, I know.

A strange, but wonderful sensation: a strong pull deep within me accompanied by small, murmuring snuffling sounds that speak of all the animal contentment in the world.

I look down on my baby's perfectly-formed miniature hands; awestruck by these unbelievably tiny fingers barely the length of the top-joint of mine yet complete with tiny wrinkles and tipped by minute tellin-shell nails with white half-moons.

The face, the hair, the body are of the moment, amorphous; they will grow and change week by week, swiftly erasing this moment's images, steadily transmuted through the stages to adulthood; the final result so 'other' that it's tempting to use the word 'metamorphosis'. But the hands! You'll see that they were so, all along. Just reduced by ten.

Fanned out on the flesh either side of the nipple they cling like a neonate kangaroo's. Wonder floods me – is an exquisite ache deep in my centre where tears well.

Blurred and choked, it comes to me with full clarity that here is resolution.

I'm not talking Motherhood. Or Fulfilment. Nor equating the one with the other.

Not at all.

The resolution is of this particular moment, is specifically mine. It so happens that in the image of this infant's head on my breast there is a fusion of two vital elements – the beauty of life and its horrors. As *I* have perceived them. My beauty. My horror. Unique to me. As are each person's dualities to themselves.

I look down on a veined white spherical thing and know it to be a part of me – grossly comic; yet too I know it to be nothing of me; a mere lump of body-matter which at the same time is, for this new-sprung creature the whole world – the supreme object of desire.

I look down and see a new beginning. My adoration is overwhelmingly fierce, tigerish in its response to the need to protect every last hair on the head of this tiny helpless creature. This feeling: so new to me, as old as time, common to a greater or lesser degree to all species who bear young.

I smile to be so very special. To be so very commonplace. Bending my neck I feel the sticky threads of mothers past lose their hold on me and drift away. I entertain the fancy of being part of that 'Queen is

Dead. Long Live the Queen!' cyclical mythical replacing.

Looking down I smile with the utmost pleasure of experiencing a sense of balance such as can equably encompass both Gulliver's disgust at the coarse-textured hairy blemished dugs of the Brobdignagian suckler and these magical globes of mine. That can rejoice in having a mouth that can at one moment pucker in revulsion at the rotten, grub-infested apple and at the next pick up and bite with delight into its neighbour. That can live in dread of any manifestation of bodily incontinence yet will cheerily clean-up the most malodorous evacuations of this creature of mine without so much as a flicker of distaste.

I look down and am consumed with the desire to cram those delicate spread fingers into my mouth, to cover every inch of this tiny mortal with great smacking kisses, to nibble the smooth pink globes of the tiny plum-like bottom. I laugh aloud with the joy of giving where there is no asking, of seeking no response. Joy that there can exist expression of such untrammelled delight unsullied by the shameful fear of thin-lipped disapproval; delight open for all the world to see.

What bliss!

What light shining into complexity's dark recesses!

There is something GLORIOUS in the state of ROUNDNESS.

31

Annie. Birthday 2000

Sixty today.

Sixty!!

God Almighty! How is that possible?

When I feel half that age? When I played five games of badminton yesterday – *singles!*

When I want to be The Dancing Queen, thresh-ing like a maenad all night long?

An OAP.

No. Not that. An *abbreviation?!* No. No way. Abbreviated I will not be. Would it be better as a word – *oap?* 'Any concessions for oaps?' … Mind, that might be heard as 'oafs'. Could go and live in sun-soaked Seville, then I'd be a jubilada. Now that's a lovely word – *jubilada.* Puts 'old-age pensioner' well and truly – and literally – in the shade! Yes. I think I could make a good stab at feeling like a jubilada in Sevilla.

Gabriel comes back with the Guardian, takes me in his arms, says kissing an old-age- pensioner was never one of his fantasies.

'What makes you think you'll get the chance?'

I dodge him and pounce on the paper.

Plastered over half the front page is a photograph of a blonde sometime-media-Babe and below that, smaller, one of a certain execrable Game-Show host – deceased. She's just found out he was her father.

Him? Good Lord! No wonder she's freaking out. I scan the revelations and turn the page. There's more! It says they're digging up what's left of that all-time star of French cinema – Yves Montand – for a paternity test.

What *is* going on?

Well, one thing that is going on is that if I'd had my wits about me I would have perceived these seeming coincidences for what they were – harbingers of doom.

The post arrives – five birthday cards. And one letter.

The letter is from Dr Barnardos.

My heart kerplunks, my face flushes, my hands go clammy before I tell myself it's much too soon for them to have checked out my case and replied to my letter. This must be a preliminary note requesting more information.

I'd watched that Barnardo's documentary. My God; when photos of the children in their care came up on the screen I didn't think I could bear to stay and see, in case …. But, of course I did stay. I couldn't not. I was literally on the edge of my seat feeling my eyes would burst from the strain of recon-ciling the urge to clamp tight-shut in huge alarm and the need to widen and devour all in an instant.

It had suddenly hit me. At any moment my face of six decades earlier – the face of me as a baby – MY FACE – could pop up large as life right in front of me on that screen, *in my living-room*. I felt nauseous, could scarcely breathe.

Then, as face after face flashed past I began to re-lax: they were all toddlers and older children whereas I had been a babe-in-arms and only in the Home for a few months.

It was so sad. Children who'd never found a home, people spending their whole lives in a search for their birth mother, their joy if they found her rarely enough to offset the years of lack. Harrowing yearned-for reunions where flaunted gladness was worried at and eroded by eddies then currents of bitter disappointment – on one side or both.

The one that really got to me was a highly successful, contented 55 year old father-of-four and grandfather. He broke down and wept with gratitude on being shown the entry telling of a 'lovely young woman' and her anguish at parting with her baby son. Single, living in poverty caring for a sick mother she'd believed she was giving her child his only chance of a decent life: 'If ever he comes to you, tell him I loved him so much and wanted more than anything on earth to keep him,' read out the counsellor in so gentle a voice. And I was weeping along with the man.

For him. For his mother. For myself. For my mother.

At the end of the programme I found myself taking down the 'Enquiries' number.

And now. This letter. In my hand.

On my sixtieth birthday.

This letter that I open with shaking hands, holding my breath.

A letter that tells me there exists no record of my having been in Dr Barnardos. Neither in residential nor in foster-care.

I'm stunned. That can't be true. How can that be? A given that I've lived with for the best part of sixty years. Not true? Apart from anything else, what about the little house. The little house! Every year my lovely little house. The constant urging to drop all my pennies into it – 'Good girl, soon be full.' Filling it to the brim till you can't get a coin-clatter when you shake it. I can see the little house to this day: its shiny cream walls, its brown-red thatch and post-box-red door. I can feel it between my two small hands – lifting, shaking, guessing all the farthings, halfpennies, pennies inside – the few frog-coloured 12-sided threepenny-bits, one or two silver sixpences, the occasional shilling. I remember the first time the Barnardo's lady came to seal and collect it I cried because she was taking it away. 'Another one will come in the post. Soon,' soothed my mum, but she didn't understand. I'd had a picture of the gummed-paper seal underneath being ceremoniously torn across and an amazing heap of shining coins spilling onto the green chenille table-cover as we watched, holding our breath – rather like the moneybags of gold Jack stole from the beanstalk Giant and emptied out before his mother's astonished gaze.

Now the ache of loss throbs in my hands as well as in my heart. Why would Mum and Dad say over and over how good Barnardo's were to me, if they weren't – if I wasn't even there? It doesn't make sense. It doesn't make sense! I feel sick inside, tears welling. It's all spoilt. Either I *was* there and Barnardo's no longer has the record – I'm not convinced by that: the reason I was tempted to write was precisely because of my amazement at their careful recording and storing of every scrap of information about every single child – or, was I cared for in the something-or-other Children's Home and mum and dad didn't like the thought of having to say 'Children's Home' to me? – or were they so taken with the word 'Doctor'? Mum bowed down before Doctors.

'Barnardo's' used generically? Like 'Hoover'? Surely that's too ludicrous?

'Get a grip, Annie.'

You go up to the bathroom.

You brush your teeth: sparingly coax out a stripey centimetre of paste onto the bristles, deftly set down the toothbrush on its spine, carefully screw its cap back on, replace it in its Blue Swallow mug, lift the brush, open wide – doing all things right, tempting no envious gods.

Then you look up into the mirror.

Bam! You're poised at the topmost point of Fortune's Wheel; you're swooping down the gamut of all the clichés – gasp, heart-lurch, flush, pupil-dilate – before you're turned to stone by the Gorgon-gaze of the mirror image.

It's not what you need.

It is *not* what you need.

On a Monday morning!

The Monday morning you turn sixty?

Transfixed I lean in close, stare and stare at the face there until my held-breath sighs out and clouds the glass. Better that it stay so but something in me won't have that and my hand fists and moves up to clear the mirror.

The sweat that broke out on sight of that mirror-image has cooled to ice. The palms of my hands are clammy.

Four words brand themselves, one by one behind my brow-bone:

He.

Was.

My.

Father.

My Dad.

He was my father.

It was him.

The breathing stops, the staring goes on, relentless: flared nostrils in a large nose, eyes brown and small, hair dark and curly, upper lip with noticeably clean-chiselled points, chin large-dimpled.

Just like him. Like Tom Pilgrim.

Like all the Pilgrims?

I run a frantic mental check of Pilgrim physiognomies – Pilgrim brothers, sisters, cousins, aunts, uncles, grandparents, desperately seeking – and finding – reassuring divergences: ocular, aural, rhinal, labial, from my own.

But the voices … the voices … Voices from my childhood, voices from those not in the know: 'My Goodness! You can certainly see who she belongs to!' – Adoptive father proudly beaming – 'You can see she's a Pilgrim all right'.

And they've all got brown eyes and dark curly hair.

Yes. And most people are totally unobservant. They always miss true likeness – especially men – all it takes is a bit of different hair or eye colouring and they spectacularly fail to discern the most striking resemblance; especially when it's a matter of face-planes rather than features. For Christ's sake, a quarter of the country's got brown eyes and dark hair. Millions of people!

Small brown eyes? *Curly* dark hair?

Leave it. *Leave* it!

But, oh, there's no shutting out the next voice – nor its accompanying image: 'Look at that then!' – My arm-chaired dad proudly indicating an hour-glass three- quarter-socked limb, muscled calf bulging above a fetlock of a singular boniness he can near-on circle with thumb and middle finger.

'Thoroughbred, me!' chortles George Pilgrim, shoeing-smith.

Now my own exaggeratedly curvaceous calves clench; a band of ice encircles, bites and numbs my similarly-thoroughbred ankles. The pupils of the mirror-face's eyes encroach on and overlay most of the iris with jet-black.

Horror. The truth has been staring me in the face all along.

Literally in the face. Numerous times a day. Since the very first time I saw myself in a mirror and knew, 'That's me.'

I see a tear form and well in each eye of the re-flected face and I feel it run down each cheek.

But … a dim, confused protest is struggling to surface … It is the wrong Nemesis! All those years the canker within was not *this* but the dreaded *Lump*. An unseen forming *within*. Not this thunderbolt come crashing from without.

But no …Oh, God! In a flash I see. What could be more *within* than this?

Only half a cuckoo-in-the-nest then?

My Father.

Him.

Laughable. Ludicrous. Absurd. Fantastic. Grotesque. Incredible. Inconceivable. Unthinkable. Out-of the-Question. Impracticable.

Impossible. Dad never went anywhere on his own except work and shooting and mending guns and things for people – and cutting the hedges of widows … And he was so strict, *that* way – sex-wise. He'd never dream of it. With an unknown eighteen year-old girl? From London? Where? How? When? Ridiculous. Preposterous.

Where would I have been born? How would Barnardo's have got me? How would I get from there to Howell – at a few months old? Where does Mrs Brown fit in? And why would he keep saying, 'She was no good. She didn't want you. She came for the money' – the litany of my childhood.

Guilty? Covering up? Quashing my mum's suspicions? Did she have suspicions?

Or. *Did she know?*

Who else knew?

Did the whole town know?

The butcher, the baker, the candlestick-maker?

Everybody but me?

Well, there's no-one left to tell me now.

So.

Do I contact an organisation? Start the search for a possibly-still-living-seventy-eight-year old woman?

After all this time?

One thing; I can't get my dad dug up like Yves Montand. Seeing as he was cremated.

Maybe do nothing? Whatever I might find out couldn't change my memories.

Leave it be.

Live for the day.

See pretty red balloons, given each birthday by the only Dad I ever knew.

See them fly high in a blue sky.

THANK YOU
for reading
See the Pretty Red Balloon.

If you enjoyed this book, please leave a review on the site where you bought it.

Reviews help other readers find books they may like.

Pentalpha Publishing Edinburgh

ABOUT THE AUTHOR

Kate Murray was born in London, evacuated to Northamptonshire, returned to London to study and stayed there for twenty years. When her children left home so did she and, with her husband, worked in France, Ireland, Germany and Spain.

Over the years her poems and stories have appeared in small magazines and anthologies, and have won prizes.

Now, still with the same husband, she lives in Edinburgh, from where from time to time she sets out on long-distance walks.

See the Pretty Red Balloon is her first novel.

38267200R00139

Printed in Poland
by Amazon Fulfillment
Poland Sp. z o.o., Wrocław